A Passionate Kiss

Sharon C. Cooper

ISBN: 978-0-9976141-3-8
Editor: Melissa Ringsted, There for You Editing
Published by: Amaris Publishing LLC in the United States
Formatted by: Enterprise Book Services, LLC

Disclaimer

This story is a work of fiction. Names, characters, and
incidents are either products of the author's imagination
or are used fictitiously. Any resemblance to actual events,
locales, organizations or persons, living or dead, is entirely
coincidental.

About the Book:

Retired Marine, Mason Bennett, has two goals: adjust to civilian life and keep drama out of it. His focus is on his role as part-owner, along with his siblings, of Atlanta's hottest nightclub. However, his attention shifts when the woman he has loved like a sister reenters his life and thoughts of a passionate kiss they shared hijacks his mind. Their connection is explosive. Feelings he's tried to deny come to the forefront, and he's tempted to do something he thought he would never do—cross that line from friends to lovers.

TV news anchor, London Alexander, is back home in Atlanta and ready to start a new chapter in her life. This time she hopes her future includes Mason, the man she has loved forever. She's ready to step over the forbidden line that he's drawn in their relationship.

Will taking a chance on love lead to a happily-ever-after? Or will risking their friendship leave them both with broken hearts?

CHAPTER ONE

"I want children, but not a wife. Why is that so hard for you to understand?" Mason Bennett dropped his head back against the high-back leather chair, irritation nipping at his nerves. He stared up at the control room's dark ceiling. "And why am I even discussing this with you?" How he and his sister ended up in this conversation was a mystery to him.

"It's a good thing we're talking about this now because clearly you have lost your mind."

Dressed to the nines in a cream-colored silk blouse and matching pants with heels too tall to be practical for walking, Harper Bennett looked as if she was on her way to a photo shoot. Instead, it was ten o'clock in the morning and she was preparing to meet with potential clients.

Mason returned his attention to the ceiling. They were hanging out in the security room of Club Masquerade, the club they owned with their brother, Cameron. Operating the hottest night club in Atlanta was no easy feat. They had inherited the business a few years ago, after their parents decided to retire and travel the country in their RV. Mason was responsible for security, while Harper organized and oversaw all events, and Cameron managed the operations of the business.

Harper released an exaggerated sigh. "Maybe you should take some more time off. Why don't—"

"I'm fine. Just because you don't agree with what I want or don't want, doesn't mean that something is wrong with me." Until a few months ago, Mason had been recuperating from injuries obtained during his last military tour in Afghanistan.

He stared at his right hand, opening and closing it, trying to work out the stiffness. He still suffered from a little achiness from time to time. Almost a year ago he'd had reconstructive surgery on the hand as well as his chin and jaw. Not a day went by that he didn't remember that time in his life—remember how he had returned home from Afghanistan broken inside and out. What he remembered most was that he'd made it back, but his best friend hadn't.

"Are you even listening to me?" His sister's voice penetrated his thoughts. She hastily pushed her long hair out of her face. "Mama would have a fit if she heard you talking like this. She might be eager for grandkids, but no way would she condone you screwing around with women only to produce a child."

Mason smiled inside. Yeah, their mother might be prissy and petite, but she wouldn't hesitate to knock him upside his head if she thought he was intentionally spreading his seed around town to produce a child.

"It's not like that." Mason still wondered why he needed to explain himself to her. "I just don't want, or intend, to do the whole relationship, commitment thing. Been there. Done that. But that doesn't mean that I don't want to be a dad. And don't worry, I'm not going to hook up with just anyone. I will definitely be selective when picking the mother of my future children."

Again, Harper frowned, looking at him as if she didn't recognize him. She crossed her arms. "Mase, what's really going on?"

Mason rubbed his hands down his jean-clad legs and glanced at one of the monitors when he saw a couple of his security specialists walk past a camera. Only a few of the monitors were currently on, displaying two of the emergency exits, and the back hall which led to the offices. Since the recent shooting in a local night club, he and his siblings realized they needed to up the club's security and had installed additional cameras. Mason had every intention of making the building as secure as possible. In a couple of months, they had plans to upgrade all of the equipment.

"Mase?" Harper ground out. "Say something. You can't really be serious about all of this."

"Dang, sis, you can quit worrying. I'm still getting acclimated to civilian life. I'm not trying to get with anyone right now."

Besides, after connecting with Faith Hanson, a woman he had dated off and on, Mason definitely wasn't looking for anything serious. They had started off in a friends-with-benefits relationship before he joined the military and hooked up whenever he was in town. A few months ago, when he decided that he was ready to have a family, he had entertained the thought of him and Faith taking their relationship to the next level. After a couple of months, he realized he couldn't handle a serious relationship, especially with her. She was still the same high maintenance, self-centered, materialistic woman she'd always been. He hated the way she treated people and she loved drama. He didn't do drama.

"You know what? You probably just need the right woman in your life and I know the perfect—"

"Stop right there. We're not in high school anymore and I'm not letting you sucker me into going out with one of your haughty girlfriends."

Harper jabbed her hands onto her hips. "My friends are not haughty!" She studied him for a long time before speaking again. "What's really going on? Does this have anything to do with the surgeries?"

"All right, I'm done talking." Mason stood abruptly, his chair rolling back, almost hitting the wall before he grabbed it. "And don't you have something you should be doing instead of getting in my business?"

Mason crawled underneath the console and went back to working on the cables for one of the monitors. He would admit that after reconstructive surgery on his face, he'd kept a low profile. But those days were in the past. These days he was just happy to be alive.

"Mase—" his sister started, but stopped when a few of his guys walked into the room laughing.

"Oh, hey, Harper," Hamilton Crosby, Mason's second in command, greeted.

"Hey guys," she mumbled, clearly not happy about the interruption. "Mason, this conversation is not over." Her heels clicked against the hardwood floor as she made a hasty exit, not bothering to wait around for a response.

"She's gone," Hamilton announced and two of the club's newest security specialists chuckled. "And you can thank us later by covering the first round of beers."

"Now that's what I'm talking about," Bones piped in. At twenty-three, he was the youngest of the security team. So far he was working out well, even though Mason could tell that he was still at the partying age.

"Consider it done. First round is on me." Rising from the floor, Mason dusted off the back of his jeans. He turned on the rest of the monitors glad to see they were all working.

"It still trips me out that you and your siblings are triplets," Bones said as everyone studied the monitors

"Yeah, we get that a lot." Mason adjusted the clarity on the monitor in front of him. He and his siblings were fraternal. Outside of their eyes and smiles, they were as different as apples and oranges.

Hamilton pointed to one of the screens tilted above their heads. "Looks like we're going to have to adjust that second camera near the front entrance." The room held a total of twenty monitors that displayed the entire 23,000 square foot facility, as well as the rooftop lounge. Whenever the club was open, they usually had four or five people monitoring the consoles at any given time.

"And the camera to the right of the circular bar needs to be adjusted," Jack added, pointing at one of the newer monitors that displayed the circular bar and the belly bar tables nearby.

"I'll take care of the one at the front entrance and Jack, you, and Bones can take care of the other one." Hamilton headed to the door, the other two guys on his heels. "Mase, let us know when they're straight."

For the next fifteen minutes they fiddled with the cameras, and adjusted a couple of others in the process.

"Ham, that's cool right there." Mason spoke into his mouthpiece. "While you're in that area, the camera closest to the …" His voice trailed off when the front door opened and a woman rushed in. What the … "Who the hell left the front door unlocked?"

Mason took in the beauty thinking there was something familiar about her. She fidgeted, rubbing her hands up and down her bare arms as she stood next to one of the two escalators. Gazing back at the entrance, it was as if she expected someone to come in after her.

Hamilton explained something to the woman, but she didn't seem to be listening. When he reached out, trying to direct her toward the door, she backed away, pointing to the escalator leading to the second and third floors.

Who is she?

Mason rubbed his chin, hoping she'd glance into the camera so he could see her face clearly. There was something so familiar about her. As if reading his mind, she turned her head slightly and he sucked in a breath. Large expressive eyes, high cheekbones, and a mouth he would never forget was on full display. He'd recognize those gorgeous lips anywhere.

But something wasn't right. Something had her spooked.

"Ham, hold up. I know her. I'm on my way," Mason said into his mouthpiece and hurried to the stairs.

He was a little surprised Hamilton hadn't recognized London Alexander, Harper's best friend. From what Mason understood, she had been to the club plenty of times when Mason's parents managed the facility and Hamilton worked security.

Seconds later, Mason slowed and London met his gaze. Guilt stabbed him in the chest. She was the last person he should be looking at with interest, but damn if she didn't look sexy in the fitted red tank top and black leggings molded around her narrow hips and shapely legs. Considering it was early afternoon on a weekday, he was surprised to see her, and in running gear at that.

"Mase," she breathed, her husky voice feeling like a feather brushing against his skin.

Mason heard a little wheezing coming from her, but she didn't look as if she was having an asthma attack, something she suffered with when they were kids. Still staring, what he couldn't get over was how different she looked. She never wore her hair super long, but the last time he'd seen her, it brushed her shoulders. Now the pixie cut transformed her whole appearance, the style seeming as if it were made for her.

When her hand went to her chest, as if trying to catch her breath, and she glanced back at the door, all of Mason's protective instincts kicked in.

"What's wrong?" He touched her arm. She was shivering. "What happened?"

She shook her head. "Nothing. I'm just surprised ... and glad to see you." She stepped closer and wrapped her arms around his waist.

Mason held her tight, but he wasn't buying her story, especially since she was trembling against him. He brushed a kiss on the side of her sweat-slicked head. Though he shouldn't be enjoying the feel of her body molded against him, he marveled at how perfectly she fit in his arms.

Still a little concerned, Mason gave a nod to Hamilton and eyed the door. The two of them had worked together long enough to read each other. Something had scared London and maybe who or what might still be out there.

*

London soaked up Mason's warmth and his familiar woodsy scent. The combination wrapped around her like a cozy blanket, making her want to snuggle even closer as a calm settled over her. God she had missed him. He felt so good, and feeling safe in his arms, she didn't want to let him go. But holding on to the man she'd had a crush on for most of her life wasn't a good idea. He thought of her as a little sister, despite the fact that they were both thirty-three and had shared a bond which wasn't brotherly or sisterly.

London drew in a deep breath and released it slowly before taking a reluctant step back. She studied Mason's handsome face. The perfectly trimmed goatee he sported was new, adding to his sexiness. Anyone who didn't know him prior to his last tour of duty, wouldn't suspect there was anything slightly different about his features. A former Marine sniper, Mason had spent several months in Germany recovering from his battle injuries before returning to the States where he needed still another surgery and even more time to recover. She would have been there for him, but he told her he didn't want her there.

Still staring at Mason, she saw there were some things about him that hadn't changed. Not only did he still favor dark colors—if his black polo shirt and dark jeans were any indication—but he was still the big, strong, sexy man she remembered. The man she loved.

London wanted to convince herself that Mason's return had nothing to do with her decision to accept the news anchor position there in Atlanta. She couldn't. His return played a major role in her relocation decision.

"It's been a long time," she finally said. *Two years.* Two years since she'd seen him. And two years since they'd shared a passionate kiss that had ruined her for any other man.

"Yeah, it has, but you didn't answer my question." He moved toward her and she stiffened, a reaction she couldn't explain. All she knew was that she was such an emotional wreck these days, if he touched her again, she might break down crying. "What's wrong?"

Sighing, London shook her head. "Nothing. I'm just … it's just …"

The security guy walked back into the room. "All clear."

"Thanks for checking, Hamilton," Mason responded without taking his gaze from her. "By the way, do you know London Alexander, Harp's best friend?"

Hamilton narrowed his eyes at her. London remembered seeing him on a couple of occasions, but never knew his name.

She gave him a slight wave. "Hi."

"Hey. Sorry about earlier. I didn't recognize you."

"Yeah, haircut." She pointed at her new hairstyle.

"And she's lost weight. Too much weight," Mason grumbled and she narrowed her eyes at him.

"Don't start," London huffed. Turning from him, she rubbed her temples, a headache lingering in the background.

"I wouldn't start if you didn't look as if you haven't eaten in weeks. Don't they have food in North Carolina? Or is that chump of a boyfriend of yours eating his food and yours, too?"

She whirled on him and punched him in the arm. "Just back off, Mason!"

"Whoa! What the hell is going on, London?" He grabbed hold of her wrist, keeping her from hitting him again. "Now I know something's wrong. Start talking."

Before she could respond, the front door opened and Mason stiffened, pulling her closer. London wondered if his reaction had something to do with his military training. For him to have sent Hamilton out to look around, he must have sensed something had freaked her out. He didn't relax until they heard keys jingling and heels clicking against the tiled floor.

"Hey, girl. I thought you were going to call …" Harper's words trailed off as she stopped in her tracks, her gaze bouncing from London to the guys. "What's going on?"

"That's what I want to know." Mason's voice dropped an octave as he maintained a loose hold on London's wrist. His grip was tender, which was more than she could say for the fire in his intense, chestnut brown eyes that were identical to Harper and Cameron's. Though they shared a birthday, the triplets were different in personality as well as looks, except for those eyes and their smiles. "London came in here shaking, looking as if she'd seen a ghost, and now she just took a swing at me."

Harper met London's gaze but remained silent as they exchanged a look. Closer than most sisters, they shared a silent language. London prayed her best friend was reading her loud and clear right now. Mason could be a hothead when he thought his family was in trouble, and ever since London was ten, the Bennetts had treated her like one of their own.

"If she hit you, you probably deserved it." Harper stuffed her keys into the side pocket of her large handbag. "Come on, girl. Let's head to my office. Mase has issues these days."

London returned her attention to him, her stare sweeping from his eyes to the hold that he still had on her wrist. "I'm fine, Mase. Really. I'm fine." She eased out of his grip.

London felt the frustration bounce off of him in waves, only making her feelings for him deepen. She knew if she ever needed anyone, he would be there. More than once he had come to her rescue and she had no doubt he still would.

Though he didn't look convinced, Mason stepped back and opened his mouth to say something, but glanced at Harper who was waiting by the escalator for her, and then at Hamilton. Instead, he turned and headed to the back of the club.

Minutes later, London strolled into Harper's office, closing the door behind her.

"Okay, what happened?" Harper asked in a rush as she set her handbag on top of her huge white desk. The pristine office decorated with French Provincial furniture was almost bigger than London's first apartment. "So?"

London roamed over to the floor to ceiling windows overlooking a wooded area. "Nothing happened. Cory has me so paranoid, I felt like I was being followed."

"What?" Harper yelled. "You think he followed you to Atlanta?"

London turned to her friend and shook her head. "No. I'm trippin'. I just had this weird feeling is all. I don't think anyone was following me."

London and Cory had parted ways almost six months ago. Against his wishes, she had moved out of the apartment—the one they'd shared in North Carolina for the past year and a half. Unfortunately, he hadn't taken their break-up well and had since started showing up at the oddest places. The last straw was when she was reporting on location in Charlotte and spotted Cory standing a few feet behind the camera man.

"Are you sure he didn't follow you to Atlanta? Considering the way he's been acting lately, I wouldn't put anything past him."

"He doesn't know I'm here." London had applied for a news anchor job at Hot Atlanta News and after two interviews, had been offered the job a few weeks ago.

"Just because you won't be on a national television station, doesn't mean Cory won't find out you're here. Maybe you should tell Mason. He has a few police officer friends in Atlanta. Perhaps there's something they can do."

London shook her head. "I told you. I talked to the police in Charlotte and they said that there's nothing they can do since Cory hasn't actually done anything. Stalking might be a crime, but he hasn't said anything to me, he hasn't sent me crazy gifts. Nothing. Whatever he's doing might not even classify as stalking. It just freaks me out a little to see him pop up at the weirdest times."

"I just don't understand that. Causing mental anguish ought to count. The way Mason was looking at you downstairs means he picked up on something. I take it you didn't tell him that you thought you were being followed."

Waving her off, London sat in one of the guest chairs facing Harper's desk. "Mase was just being his usual over-protective self."

"Maybe that's good. You could be in danger for all we know. And clearly Cory's antics are stressing you out. Look at you." Harper put her hand on her hip. "You've lost at least ten pounds—weight you didn't have to lose, I might add—since I saw you two months ago."

"I know. There's just been a lot going on and I haven't had much of an appetite. I have a lot on my mind." And seeing Mason added to the knots twisting in her stomach. She thought that after all of these years, her feelings for him would have subsided, but that definitely wasn't the case. If anything, each time she was near him, her feelings grew more intense.

Harper glanced at her watch and pulled a file from the bottom drawer of her desk. "So what's been on your mind? You did sound a little strange the other day when we talked, but I thought you were just anxious about the new job."

"That, and I've been thinking about my life." London toyed with the diamond-shaped, crystal paperweight on the desk. "You were right when you told me I needed to buckle down and start thinking more about my future. I feel different. Everything seems to be changing around me, but I'm stuck in a rut. And I've missed you guys."

London's grandparents, the Bennetts' neighbors, took her in twenty years ago after her parents were killed, and raised her. Three years ago they passed away within months of each other, leaving London alone. Heartbroken and wallowing in grief, London thought getting out of Atlanta was the answer.

"I'm ready to settle down and have a family," she whispered more to herself than to Harper. "Most of our friends are married with one or two children and I'm just …" She shrugged without finishing. Her emotions had been all over the place since she accepted the job in Atlanta. Arriving in town last night she'd been excited, but it was as if a dark cloud hovered above her, bringing with it a depression she hadn't felt in years.

Harper went around the desk, sat on the arm of the chair, and hugged London. "I know the last few years have been hard, but I'm glad you're back. You need to be around family. And before you say you don't have any family, you know you do. We will always be here for you."

"I know."

"You're my sister and Cameron feels the same way. As for Mason, you already know how he feels about you."

London released an unladylike snort. "Yeah, he thinks of me as a kid sister … still."

Harper straightened and smoothed down her blouse. They'd been friends forever, and for as long as London could remember, her friend always looked perfectly pulled together, even when they were kids. She refused to wear anything except the latest fashions and that hadn't changed.

"You and Mason are in denial." Harper reclaimed her seat. "I've seen the way you two look at each other. I don't know why you can't see how much he loves you, and Mason can't seem to admit how he feels about—" A knock sounded at the door, interrupting Harper. "Come in."

A tall kid—wearing a white shirt, with a black tie hanging loose around his neck, and black slacks—strolled in. The club was closed, but London assumed that he was part of Club Masquerade's security team since black suits were required attire when they were on duty at the club.

The guy moved farther into the room with a toothy smile and carrying a brown paper bag. It must have been filled with food if the enticing sweet and spicy aromas suddenly permeating the office were any indication. "I take it you're London." He stood next to her chair and London glanced from him to Harper and then back at him.

"May … be," she said slowly.

Harper grinned and pointed at the paper bag. "What's in the bag, Bones?"

"Mase told me to bring this up to London. He said she was in your office, so I assumed …" He shrugged. "Anyway, he said and I quote, 'Eat. You need to put some meat on those bones.'"

Harper burst out laughing and London rolled her eyes even though she was touched by his gesture. Smiling, she accepted the bag.

"Well, you can tell him he needs to mind his own business."

"Oh, and Harp, Mase said there's enough for you, but don't eat up everything from London." Bones left the office laughing, closing the door behind him.

"See, I told you. Mase is in love with you. Do you think he would do this for anyone else?" Harper grabbed plates and utensils from the cabinet near the round table that she used for talking with clients.

London strolled across the room and set the bag on the table. She didn't know what to make of Mason's gesture. Granted, he always looked out for her when they were kids, and even before he joined the Marines, but they hadn't spent much time together in years. Why would he even bother? He hadn't accepted any of her calls while he was recovering in Germany. And he didn't want her to visit once he arrived back in the States. Harper claimed that he was self-conscious about his scars, but London wasn't buying it. He didn't want anything to do with her and she was okay with that … well, until today. Until she saw him and he held her in his arms.

London pulled containers out of the bag and her hand went to her chest realizing he'd gotten her Thai food, her favorite. "I can't believe he remembered," she murmured quietly.

"You know I hate to say it, but I told you so. And, girl, let me tell you about the crazy conversation he and I had earlier. He said he wants children, but not a wife. Can you believe that nonsense?"

London ate and listened as her friend talked about why intentionally having children out of wedlock was a bad idea. Yet, London could understand Mason's reasoning. Though she wanted to get married and have a family one day soon, she'd consider foregoing marriage to have children with the right man.

CHAPTER TWO

"Harper, we're not increasing the budget for you to buy more furniture for the VIP section. That's ridiculous. The sofas are only a year old and they still look brand new." Cameron's voice cut into Mason's thoughts.

For the past hour, Mason had been sitting in Cameron's office with him and Harper discussing some budget changes. Unfortunately, if he was quizzed on what had been discussed, he'd fail. His mind kept wandering back to London.

It had been three days since he'd seen her and not a minute had gone by that he hadn't thought about her. Something was very wrong and he intended to find out what. Besides that, seeing her had conjured up memories of the night they'd shared that brain-jarring kiss.

It was a Thanksgiving Day and he'd been on leave. His mother always went all out for the holidays, and even more so on those rare occasions when he was able to join the family. Throughout that day, he and London had skirted around each other. Mason wasn't sure what it was, but she looked different to him. She was no longer his sister's pesky sidekick. When she got ready to leave, he had walked her out to her car, something he'd done more times than he could count over the years. It was like any other time until she surprised the hell out of him when her lips touched his. He and London had always had a special bond—one he couldn't explain—but he never considered that bond to be a romantic one … until that day.

They had never crossed that line. A line that couldn't be physically seen but was drawn to keep a man from longing for a woman who he'd always considered a sister. Until that night. A night and a kiss he would never forget. That night, everything changed.

"Does that work for you, Mase?"

Mason's gaze shot up to find Cameron and Harper staring at him.

Sighing, his brother leaned back in his seat. "You're the one who wanted all of us to meet and you're not even paying attention. Are we keeping you from something?"

"Or from someone," Harper cracked, a grin inching across her lips.

Mason was still a little ticked at her for not telling him what was really going on with London. She could be so tight-lipped at times. All she said was that London had recently moved back to Atlanta, which was news to him. Yet another secret his sister had kept. She also mentioned London had a lot going on because of the move. However, Mason knew there was more. There was something that she and London weren't telling him.

"Does what work for me?" he asked Cameron. No sense in acting as if he knew what they'd been talking about because he didn't have a clue.

"For this year, we have an additional $12,000 we can put toward upgrading the security system and another

$40,000 to add three more armed guards on the weekends. I know you asked for more, but—"

"We'll make it work," Mason cut in. He had a few friends on the police force and had offered them the part-time gig for when they were off duty. He wanted to see how it worked out using Atlanta's finest since he was in negotiations with a friend who was looking to expand his security business to Atlanta.

"What's going on, Mason?" Cameron closed the file in front of him and set his pen down next to it. "You usually don't say much in these meetings, but damn, man. You're even more tense than you were when you first got back. Are you okay?"

Harper tapped her nails against the tabletop, drawing Mason's attention.

"Ask Harp. Something is going on with London. I have a feeling it's something serious."

Cameron looked pointedly at Harper. Though they were triplets, Harper and Mason always looked to him as the big brother with all the answers. Maybe because he had been born first. Either way, Cameron fell easily into the role.

"What's up with London?" Cameron's authoritative, no nonsense tone left no doubt that now he was concerned. Harper remained silent, gnawing on the tip of her thumbnail as if debating on whether or not to tell them. Her silence only made Mason more anxious. "She's our sister, too, Harp. If she's in trouble, we need to know. We can't help her if you two aren't telling us what's going on."

When the Bennetts first met London, sitting on her grandparents' porch, she was a super skinny, very shy ten-year-old. Though she and Harper connected immediately, London shied away from Mason. After a while she warmed to him and Cameron, and they started picking on her the same way they harassed Harper. But when Mason was around thirteen, his feelings for her started changing and the attraction only grew.

"Well?" Cameron prompted, but Harper still said nothing.

Mason jerked out of his chair. "Dammit, Harper. Now I know somethings going on! Is she in trouble? Is she in danger? What?"

"Fine!" Harper huffed, folding her arms across her chest. "Her ex-boyfriend has been harassing her."

"What?" Mason yelled. "Someone is harassing her and you didn't think it was important to tell us? How long has this been going on? And is this the asshole she was living with?"

Harper nodded. "She's going to kill me for telling you guys, especially you, Mason."

"What? Why?" Bracing his hands on the table, he stared at his sister. "Why wouldn't she want me to know?"

Cameron stood and grabbed his suit jacket from the back of his desk chair. "I can't believe you even have to ask that."

Now Mason was really confused. "What?"

"Remember Jasper Hart from high school?" Harper asked. She and Cameron looked at him pointedly.

Yeah, Mason remembered the punk. He had transferred to their high school during their sophomore year and took a liking to London. There hadn't been a problem until she told Jasper she wasn't interested in him. The guy didn't take rejection well and started picking on her and talking trash to his friends about what he had supposedly done with her. And then Mason found out. He'd caught the guy one day after school and beat his ass.

"Don't even try denying that you beat him up and broke his arm," Cameron said. "He might have told everyone that he fell off of his skateboard, but I saw you."

Mason's brows shot up. "How? When?"

"I was following him ..." Cameron shrugged. "Let's just say I had the same intentions."

"Are you serious?" Harper gasped. "With Mason I wasn't surprised since he used to be a fight first ask questions later kinda guy, but you, Cam?"

Mason grinned at his brother. "I guess great minds think alike." They shared a fist bump. "But how did you know?" Mason asked Harper.

"Me and London were at our lockers one day after school and Jasper got in her face. Told her that if she ever sicced her boyfriend, Mase, on him again, he was going to the principal and then to the cops."

"Damn, she never said anything," Mason said more to himself than to anyone else.

He opened and closed his hand trying to work out the stiffness. "Why didn't she tell me?"

"She vowed then that she was never telling you if anyone bothered her. She was afraid you'd get into trouble and end up in jail."

"Hell, we were kids, Harp. I was only watching her back."

No telling what London would have done had she known about the other guys he had handled on her behalf in high school. Cute, tiny, and introverted at the time, she was like a magnet, drawing the attention of the guys in their class, especially the jocks. Back then, Mason had made it his personal mission to watch out for her.

"Now is different," he said with conviction. "This situation is different."

He was different. He and London hadn't spent much time together lately, but that didn't make her any less important to him. Trying to get her to talk to him before she left the club the other day had been futile. She thanked him for lunch and left. Clearly she was still pissed that he hadn't wanted to see her after his accident. It wasn't so much that he hadn't wanted to see her; it was because he hadn't been in a good place. Losing his best friend, Andre, in the same explosion that had ripped off part of Mason's face and damaged his hand, had rocked him to the core. He hadn't really wanted to talk to anyone after that.

"So what are we going to do about this boyfriend?" Cameron asked Mason.

"Ex-boyfriend," Mason corrected absently, wondering what to do with this newfound information. "We aren't going to do anything, but I'm going to talk to London."

"You can't." Rising, Harper gathered her papers. "Because then she's going to know I told you."

"I won't tell her. Where is she right now?" Mason headed to the door.

"She's at my place. What are you going to do?"

"I'm just going to talk to her. Hopefully I can get her to tell me about this guy."

*

London switched her cell phone to her other ear. She stood at the kitchen counter in Harper's loft listening as her realtor went on and on about the places she had shown London the day before.

"And I have a few more homes I can show you tomorrow. There's an adorable little craftsman-style house that came on the market this morning which meets all of your requirements."

Pulling the phone away from her ear, London stared at it. How many times did she have to keep repeating herself to this real estate agent?

"Cynthia, I told you. I don't want a single family house, and I don't want a townhouse. I'm only interested in condos or an apartment in a secured building. That's it."

London glanced around Harper's home. The woman loved her white. London wouldn't mind something like her friend's two bedroom, two bath loft, but definitely a different color pallet. Unfortunately, London couldn't afford something like this. Much of her money was tied up until she turned thirty-five and she didn't want to be house poor.

"Are you sure, dear?" Cynthia pulled London back into the conversation. "I thought you'd want something like what you grew up in. Your parents' home was—"

Emotion suddenly clogged London's throat and tears pricked the back of her eyes. "Cyn-Cynthia, I don't think this is going to work out. Thanks for your help." London hung up before the woman could say anything more. She set her cell phone on the white, quartz kitchen counter and covered her mouth with her hand, trying to hold back a sob.

Tomorrow would be twenty-three years since her parents' death. She knew returning to Atlanta at this time of the year was a bad idea, but she thought she could handle it. She thought she had dealt with her demons. She thought she had cried her last tear for what happened to them. Yet, just the mention of a single family house and her parents in the same conversation felt as if someone had punched her in the chest.

"No tears," she mumbled and swiped at her eyes. "I'm done cr—"

She startled when the intercom buzzed. Anxiousness coursed through her veins and her mind went immediately to thoughts of Cory. There was no way he'd found her. As far as she knew, he still thought she lived in North Carolina.

Wiping her face with the back of her hand, London hurried to the intercom.

"Yes?"

"London, it's me." Mason's deep, sensual voice sent a shiver through her body.

She stepped back wondering what he was doing there. Besides that, he and Cameron had access to the building and a key to the loft, so she was a little surprised that he didn't use it. Then again, maybe it was good he called up first. Otherwise, she probably would have had a heart attack if he'd just walked in.

Without responding, she buzzed him in. Taking a quick glance in the mirror near the door, she cringed at the redness in her eyes and her lack of makeup. With no intentions of leaving the house, she hadn't bothered with makeup and dressed in the first tank top and shorts her hands landed on.

"Oh well, there's nothing I can do now." She wiped her face again before finger combing her short hair. A quick glance at the clock and she saw that it was late afternoon and she wondered why he wasn't at the club. Then again, he was one of the owners. He probably set his own schedule.

She jumped and her heart lurched at the two quick knocks against the door.

Geesh, she was jumpy. With the events of the last few weeks, her nerves were fried. And now she had to be in the presence of Mason which would no doubt send her pulse racing like an out of control train down a track.

"Relax," she told herself, "it's just Mase."

Just Mase. Ha! For her that was like saying it was *just* President Barack Obama at the door. Even as children, there was something about Mason that had always sent her nerves into overdrive.

Blowing out a breath, she readied herself before swinging the door open. Warmth soared through her veins. As expected, every cell in her body went on high alert and her heart beat triple time at the sight of him. Leaning against the door jamb, looking sexier than any man had a right to, Mason acted as if he didn't have a care in the world. Baseball cap pulled low over his eyes, a long sleeved, striped shirt with the two top buttons undone, and a pair of dark jeans that fit him perfectly, only added to his sexiness.

"You gon' invite me in or just continue checking me out?"

Heat rose to London's cheeks and she swallowed hard. "Oh, sorry." She stepped back, opening the door wider. While practically drooling over him, she had totally missed the large pizza box he walked in with.

"What are you doing here, Mason?"

"I came to check on you." Setting the box down on the counter, he gave her a once over. His appreciative gaze lingered a little longer on her bare legs, making her fidget under his inspection. "Have you eaten?"

She started to lie, but instead shook her head.

He narrowed his eyes. "Are you telling me that you haven't eaten all day? It's almost four o'clock."

"Mase, if you came over here to give me a hard time, save it. I'm not in the mood." London pushed away from the door, bumping his arm as she strolled past him and into the living room. She plopped down on the sofa, folding her legs beneath her. A little surprised that he didn't follow her, she picked up the remote and pointed it at the television. She wasn't used to being home in the middle of the day, but she was happy for the downtime before she started her new job in a few days. The plan was to stay with Harper for a while until she found a place to either lease or buy. But first she had to get herself together. She was an emotional wreck.

London clicked through the channels until she landed on a talk show. Setting the remote on the table, she glanced up just as Mason walked in carrying a tray in one hand and the pizza box in the other.

"Here." He handed her the tray, which held two plates and napkins, while he set the box on the table in front of the sofa. "What do you want to drink?"

"Water is fine."

Her stomach growled when she lifted the lid on the pizza box and her heart melted. First Thai food the other day and now another favorite, lasagna pizza.

Could Harper be right about Mason's feelings for me? London shook the ridiculous thought out of her head. No way did feeding her mean that a man was in love with her. Or did it?

London shook her head again. Mason might've been the most thoughtful man she knew, but he'd made his feelings for her clear. They could never be more than friends.

She placed a slice of pizza on each plate, her mouth watering in anticipation. She couldn't read too much into his gesture. Even though they were just friends, he had always watched out for her, making her feel special. She had missed him like crazy those first few years after he had enlisted in the Marine Corp. He had call her occasionally when he was stationed in Jacksonville, but she rarely heard from him once he left for Afghanistan.

"You know Harper would have a fit if she knew we were eating in the living room, right?" Mason set their drinks on the coasters.

"I know. I'm trusting you to do what you do so well."

"And what's that?"

"Keep your mouth shut."

Chuckling, he sat next to her with his own tray. "I won't tell if you don't."

"So why are you here?" she asked, biting into a slice of pizza. Her eyes drifted closed as she savored the combination of spicy, well-seasoned meat mixed with a remarkable sauce and ricotta and Romano cheese. All of that on top of the hand-tossed crust that delighted her taste buds. She hadn't had pizza in months and having a slice from her favorite pizza joint was like winning the lottery. She brought the slice to her mouth again.

"You were on my mind."

Her hand stalled, the pizza only an inch from her lips. London set the slice on the plate and placed it on the table.

"Why was I on your mind?"

He shrugged as he finished chewing. "I keep thinking about the other day at the club. Something wasn't right. I don't know what spooked you, but fear was written on your face when you rushed into the club. Tell me what's going on."

London sat mute. She appreciated his concern, but …

"London, talk to me." Mason set his empty plate on the table.

She wiped her mouth with one of the napkins and stood, but Mason stopped her with a hand on her arm.

London shivered at his touch. The other day hadn't been a fluke. Everything within her still came alive when Mason looked at her or touched her.

She stared into his sexy eyes and sighed, dropping back down on the sofa. Suddenly she wasn't hungry.

"I told you, I don't want to talk."

"Why not?"

"Mason, please." Sitting back against the sofa, she shut her eyes and realized how tired she was. "Normally you're the one who sits around brooding in silence. So why are you trying to get me to talk?"

"'Cause normally I can't get you to shut up. So forgive me if your silence is putting me on edge." She felt him move closer and rest his arm behind her on the back of the sofa. "Talk to me, Tiny."

Her eyes popped opened and she lifted her head. London had spent a lot of time with all of the Bennetts, but Mason held her heart. He was her protector, always watching over her. And as kids, he was the only person who called her Tiny. He hadn't used the nickname since high school.

Mason massaged the back of her neck and London moaned, unable to help herself. His strong but soothing hands offered just enough pressure. If he knew how turned on he was making her, he would stop. Then again, maybe he wouldn't.

Minutes passed without either of them speaking. There was so much clogging her mind these days, if she was going to talk, she wouldn't know where to start.

"Tomorrow is the anniversary of my parents' murder," she blurted. "When those assholes stormed into our house and shot them point blank."

Mason's hand stilled and he cursed under his breath. "Ah, baby, I'm sorry. I forgot."

She didn't expect him or anyone else to remember. Heck, she'd tried for years to forget the night two armed men burst into her parents' home. The night when gunfire exploded on the first floor while she was in the basement's rec room. The night that she hid on the side of the dryer fearing that they were going to come after her next.

"For some reason, lately, I've been wondering if there was more I could have done. I should have done more, but I just hid. I didn't call 911. I didn't go up to see if I could scare those men away. I did nothing but hide."

"Tiny, you were a child. Your parents would have wanted you to do exactly what you did. Your grandfather told you that all the time. Why are you questioning this now?"

London shook her head. This time of year, she always thought about the what ifs of that night. Deep in her heart she knew that there wasn't much she could have done. Sometimes in her dreams she could hear her mother say, "Stay downstairs."

"Come here." Mason pulled London against the side of his body and held her close. "What can I do?"

There was nothing he could do. There was nothing anyone could do.

Feeling a tightness in her throat and tears pricking the back of her eyes, London buried her head against Mason's chest. She didn't want to cry. She didn't want to feel anymore. But ...

Unable to stop the pain in her heart, tears streamed down her face. Her world as she knew it had changed that night.

CHAPTER THREE

Unsure of how else to comfort London, Mason held her close. No one deserved to endure the type of pain she had lived through. And some asshole harassing her was probably making life even harder to deal with. Mason still needed her to tell him what was going on with her ex-boyfriend.

She felt perfect in his arms. He didn't want to let her go. He was glad he could be there for her, but on the other hand, she felt too good, her soft body molded …

"I'm sorry." London sat up and wiped her eyes, trying to pull away, but he held on.

"You have nothing to be sorry about."

"It's been a tough couple of weeks. I'm probably just tired." She rested her head back against his chest.

Mason grabbed one of Harper's sofa pillows, not caring that she'd have a fit if she knew what he was about to do with it. Placing the pillow on his lap, he patted it.

"Why don't you stretch out and try to get a little sleep."

London straightened, her gaze meeting his. "Don't you have to go to work?"

He shook his head. "Nope. Besides, even if I did, I think you need me more."

Her shoulders drooped and her eyes filled with more tears.

"What? What did I say?"

"You always say the right thing ... or do the right thing. I just—"

"Come on. Lie down. You're just tired. Once you get some sleep, you'll remember all the ways I used to get on your nerves."

"You're probably right." She wiped her face and stretched her legs out on the sofa. Laying on the pillow, she said, "I'm glad you're here."

"Yeah, me too. Now go to sleep."

Mason grabbed the television remote and turned to Sports Center, glad he didn't have to go to the club. Even on some of his nights off, he dropped by to see how things were going. But right now there was no other place he'd rather be.

He glanced down when London's soft snores penetrated his thoughts. She hadn't been lying down for five minutes and already she seemed to be in a deep sleep. Watching her brought back memories of them as kids, when she'd spend the night over their house. Despite the twin beds in Harper's room, sometimes in the middle of the night, she would sneak across the hall and climb into his bed.

Back then they were so young, it wasn't a big deal. He would just scoot over and they both would fall back to sleep. It wasn't until he was around thirteen or fourteen that his body started changing, making it weird to share a bed. Still, that didn't stop her from coming into his room claiming she couldn't sleep. During those times, he would wait until she fell asleep and then he would make a pallet on the floor next to bed for himself.

But now? Now she was a beautiful, grown woman who he couldn't stop staring at. Baby smooth skin, naturally long lashes which brushed the top of high cheekbones. And that mouth. Lips that had shown up in his dreams on more than one occasion since the Thanksgiving night they had shared their first and only kiss.

His gaze went lower. He took in her slim but shapely body and remembered how good she had felt in his arms moments ago, as well as the other day at the club. She fit so perfectly—as if she'd been made for him.

Blowing out a breath, Mason shook his head. He had to stop seeing her as a woman and remember that she was family. London didn't have her parents or her grandparents any longer, but he would make sure that she always had him.

He slouched down and rested his head against the back of the sofa, placing his arm around her narrow waist. The need to hold her was almost overwhelming. Hopefully, though sleep, she could feel how much he cared for her. Being there with her seemed normal. Eating their favorite meal, snuggled on the sofa and watching highlights of last night's NBA game. Yep, this felt right to him. Too bad there could never be anything more between them.

Hours later, London whimpered in her sleep, and then shifted onto her side facing him. Her eyes were still closed, but she moved again, snuggling closer. She'd been asleep for the past four hours and hadn't even awakened when he slid from beneath her to clean up before his sister arrived home. Nor did she wake up when Harper ran in to change clothes before heading right back out.

London shifted again, turning onto her back. Her tank top twisted just under her breasts, revealing flat abs and smooth, caramel skin. Unable to resist, Mason ran his hand over her stomach. The moment he touched her soft skin, he knew he'd made a mistake. This woman was like his kryptonite, weakening his defenses. For years he'd been able to remember that she was like a sister to him, but not lately. His feelings for her were definitely not brotherly and he had no clue of what to do about that.

London's mouth slid open and she released a noisy yawn as she stretched her arms up and out. When her right hand bumped his chest, she gasped and leapt up.

"Aargh!" she screamed when she turned suddenly, almost falling off the sofa.

"Whoa. I got you." He gripped her tighter, keeping her from falling.

She scurried into a sitting position. "Wha…what are you doing here?"

Mason narrowed his eyes. "You don't remember letting me in?" He studied her, now even more concerned. Though she appeared to be wide awake, the dark circles under her eyes made it look as if she was still tired.

She shook her head and sat back. "Yeah. Yeah, I remember. I don't know why I … What time is it?"

"Almost nine o'clock."

"Wow, I must have been more tired than I thought." Yawning, she rubbed the back of her neck. "Is Harper here?"

"Nah. She left about an hour ago. She had a date."

"Oh."

Sadness covered her features and Mason tugged on the hem of her tank top.

"What else is bothering you? Clearly you haven't been eating and you haven't been sleeping. I have a feeling this is not just about your parents."

"The last few weeks have been a little stressful. I guess everything is starting to catch up with me."

"Everything like what?"

She twisted her lip between her teeth, something she used to do often when deep in thought or nervous.

"You know you can talk to me, right?"

Lifting her gaze to him, London slowly nodded. "I've been trying to find a place to stay but made the mistake and picked a realtor who was a friend of my parents. She's been trying to show me everything I don't want, like single family homes and town homes."

Since the home invasion, London had been afraid of staying in single family homes alone. When she lived with her grandparents, she never stayed by herself. If they weren't going to be there, she was next door at their house hanging out. That went on through high school, and as an adult she still was afraid.

"The pressure of starting a new job in a few days isn't helping. I'm excited about being a news anchor, but I'm nervous, too. It's a lot different than being a field reporter."

"I have no doubt that you're going to be great." Mason rubbed her arm, but moved his hand away. He wanted to be there for her, at least until she got settled, but it was going to be hell on his self-control.

London leaned forward and wrung her hands, as if debating on whether or not to tell him what was really on her mind.

"What else?"

"Cory and I broke up a few months ago."

"Good," Mason mumbled. "I never liked that guy anyway."

"You didn't even know him. You only saw him in a picture and that was two years ago."

"And I could tell he was a loser. You should've listened to me when I told you that." Granted he wouldn't like anyone she dated, but there was something about the guy's eyes that didn't sit right with Mason. "So what happened? What made you finally come to your senses?"

London stood abruptly, tugged down the tale of her shirt, and strolled out of the living room. Mason watched the gentle sway of her hips in the too short shorts and his shaft shifted. Damn his body for responding to her, especially now. He had stopped by to get her to tell him what was going on, not to ogle her and dream about what it would be like to feel her body beneath him.

Dammit. This has to stop.

Mason was slow to follow her into the kitchen. He stood back as she rinsed her hands in the sink, still no response to his question from moments ago.

What the heck had this guy done to make her clam up like this? The longer it took her to tell him what was going on, the more his protective instincts amped up.

Mason walked up behind her, blocking her in with his arms on either side of her. "Did he do something to you?" Her subtle fragrance, a mixture of some type of flower and baby powder enticed him when he lowered his head, only inches from her ear. "Talk to me. I'm worried about you."

She blew out a breath and turned, but he didn't step back. His gaze went to her pouty lips and the urge to taste her was stronger than ever. The restraint he'd used

35

whenever in her presence was weakening. She wasn't supposed to look this good to him.

His brain told him to take two steps back, but his body wouldn't budge.

Damn, he had it bad.

"Mason, if I tell you what's been going on, will you promise to stay out of it?"

His jaw twitched involuntarily and he gripped the edge of the counter tighter. "No. Seeing how tired you are and how thin you've gotten I can't make that type of promise. At least not until I know what happened."

She sighed loudly and pushed against his chest to move him back, but he stayed put. He wasn't moving or leaving that loft until he found out what was troubling her. If it took all night, so be it.

*

Frustration roared through London's body. She couldn't handle Mason's closeness. When he first left for the military, she thought her heart would split in two. She had loved him from a distance and regretted that she hadn't told him how she felt back then.

Who was she kidding? Had she come clean back then, he probably wouldn't have believed her anyway.

London glanced up at him and her heart rate sped up. His unyielding gaze bore into her, waiting for her to say something. She struggled to get her mind to work, his presence and the lack of space between them wreaking havoc on her senses. Something was definitely wrong with her. Heat engulfed her body and he hadn't even touched her.

Her gaze dropped to his full, kissable lips, tempting her to reach up and pull his face close.

Oh what the hell.

She grabbed a handful of his shirt and pulled him within an inch of her mouth. He didn't resist. Was it possible that they were thinking the same thing? Did he want to taste her as much as she wanted to taste him?

No longer caring about the consequences, London's lips touched his tentatively at first, but he quickly took over. He wrapped his arm around her waist and crushed her to him, taking what he wanted ... what they both wanted. She melted into his embrace, enjoying the passion they both couldn't deny any longer.

Every emotion London ever felt for him came to the forefront and her knees weakened. His tongue explored the recesses of her mouth, sending shivers racing through her. God she loved this man. Everything about Mason from his gentleness when dealing with her to his signature woodsy cologne. Add his sharp mind and strong, powerful body, and he was everything she wanted and more.

The way their bodies responded to each other was a sign that the kiss years ago hadn't been a fluke. Deep in London's soul she knew back then the attraction between them was real. Now she was absolutely sure. All she had to do was show him that what he felt wasn't sisterly love. No way could he kiss her like this and think of her as a sister. Impossible.

How many times had she dreamt about what it would be like to feel his mouth against hers again? Taste his sweet lips. She longed to be in his arms like this, his hard body rubbed up against hers.

Her hands slid up his arms, gripping his thick biceps while one of his hands went behind her neck, pulling her even closer. Their kiss deepened and a moan filled the quiet space. London didn't know if it came from him or from her. All she knew was that she wanted more. She wanted him. All of him.

She whimpered when he eased his lips from hers and touched his forehead to hers. Breathing heavily, they stayed that way for the longest until he lifted his head.

"That was a hell of a distraction and I'd be lying if I said that I didn't enjoy it." Nuzzling her neck, he planted a sweet kiss on her cheek before touching her lower lip with the tip of his finger. "But I still want answers. I'm not leaving here until I get them. When someone messes with my family, I want to know." He straightened and his hands went back to gripping the counter, locking her in place.

"Mase."

"What has that asshole done to you?"

"Grrr, Mason!" She pounded his chest with a closed fist. "Just leave it alone."

Why had she kissed him? She was definitely losing it if she thought a simple kiss would get him to see her as a woman, and not his sister. He had told Harper he wasn't the relationship type and that he wasn't looking for one, which went against everything London wanted. Not only did she want him to see her as a woman, but she wanted him to see her as *The One*. The one he thought about morning, noon, and night. The one he couldn't live without. The one he wanted as the mother of his children.

But that was never going to happen, and the sooner she got it through her thick head, the better she would be.

"Lon—"

"I can't tell you."

"Dammit, London. Why not?"

"Because you might hurt him and …"

"And what?"

"And I don't want you to do anything that will make you end up in jail! He's not worth it. He's a non-entity at this point."

"Let me be the judge of that. As far as me getting into trouble … depending on what he's done, that might not be an issue. But we won't know until you tell me what the hell is going on."

London lowered her head, her chin touching her chest. Mason had always come to her rescue whether she wanted him to or not, but they weren't kids anymore. He was a trained killer and could probably take Cory out with one arm tied behind his back.

Mason lifted her chin with his finger and their gazes locked. "I can take care of myself," he said as if reading her mind. "You're important to me, London. You're family."

Frustration jockeyed around in her gut. Therein lie the biggest problem. She wasn't his family and so help her if he said anything about her being like a sister, she was going to throat punch him.

"Talk."

Sighing loudly, she folded her arms. "He um …" She felt Mason stiffen. *This is a bad idea.*

"He what?" Mason asked impatiently. "You either tell me what the hell he's done or what he's doing to you, or I will find that motherfu—"

"He was stalking me. Sort of."

"Sort of? What the hell does that mean? He's either stalking you or not. Has he hurt you?"

"No. He hasn't physically done anything to me since …"

London startled when Mason held her chin between his finger and thumb, his face only inches from hers. His touch was light, gentle, but the look in his gorgeous

39

brown eyes was anything but. "He put his hands on you? He hit you?"

London wanted to avert her gaze, but couldn't. Having Mason so close to her, touching her, staring into her eyes had her brain malfunctioning.

"No," she finally said, and his eyes softened. "He pushed me against a wall because he thought I was cheating on him, but he didn't hit me."

The hardness in Mason's eyes returned. London wanted to tell him that though she never cheated on Cory, her heart didn't belong to him. She loved only one man.

"Were you?"

Her eyebrows pinched together. "Was I what?"

"Cheating?"

"Does it matter?"

Dropping his hand, Mason stepped back. "No. It doesn't. You said he was stalking you. Did you go to the police?"

"They said there was nothing they could do since he hadn't done anything. After I moved out of our place, he would just show up at the oddest times. At the grocery story, when I was leaving work, or whenever I was on assignment, he would be there. He had to be following me or had someone following me. That's the only way he could have known where I was or what I was doing. It had gotten to the point I was afraid to go anywhere by myself, worried he might be there. But he never touched me or said anything. He would just look at me."

Mason turned and rubbed the back of his neck. With his right hand, he balled it into a fist and then opened it slowly. She had noticed the same movement earlier, and wondered if he was massaging his war injury.

"For the record, I didn't cheat on Cory. I just never loved him. Toward the end of our relationship, I wasn't even sure if I liked him. I stayed with him because …" She shrugged. "I'm not sure why I stayed. I guess … I guess I just didn't want to be alone," she said quietly, hating that she was one of those women. She couldn't have the man she wanted and settled for less than she deserved.

Mason turned to her. "Baby, you will never be alone. You'll always have me, Cam, and Harp. And my folks love you like their own."

London shook her head. "I know, and I love you guys. But, Mason, sometimes a woman needs more."

"I understand wanting more."

When he didn't elaborate, London moved past him and opened the refrigerator, pulling out the pitcher of iced tea she'd made earlier that day. She grabbed a glass from the cabinet near the sink.

"Do you want some?"

"Nah, I'm good." He leaned against the breakfast bar, legs crossed at the ankle. His gaze followed her every move.

"Did you return to Atlanta because of Cory?"

She took a sip of her tea thinking about how to answer the question. "He's part of the reason."

After that Thanksgiving night, when Mason told her they could never be more than friends, she started dating Cory exclusively. Before then, they went out a few times, but it was nothing serious. After dating for almost two years, he started talking marriage. London kept stalling, hoping what she felt for him would turn into love. That never happened. When she finally broke things off with Cory and packed up to leave, he made it clear he wasn't giving up on their relationship.

London sipped her tea, trying to ignore the intensity in Mason's eyes. She was ready to settle down and have a family, but not with Cory. She didn't know how she could move on until she dealt with her feelings for the handsome man standing across from her. Loving Mason affected every relationship she ever had—which only intensified after they shared that kiss right before he left for his last tour in Afghanistan.

Thoughts of what Harper told her about him wanting children, but not a wife, floated around in London's mind. Could she really consider an arrangement like that?

"What's the other reason you moved back?"

London hesitated. Should she tell him that she was madly in love with him and could barely think straight whenever she was near him? No, she couldn't. He'd run and their friendship would be non-existent. She couldn't risk that. She wouldn't.

"I wanted to come home. I missed you guys and I needed a change. I'm ready to start the next chapter of my life."

Mason remained silent. He had never been a big talker and according to Harper, since he'd returned to Atlanta, he talked even less. London wondered if it was because of the things he'd seen in the war. Or did it have something to do with losing his friend during the same accident that had injured him?

"I was sorry to hear about Andre," London said, changing the subject. "I know you guys were close." Andre Gibbs and Mason had enlisted in the military at the same time. They were as close as brothers. London would never forget when the family got word that there had been an accident. Mason had survived, but not Andre.

"Thanks." Mason rubbed his hand.

"Is your hand bothering you?"

"It's a little stiff."

"Have you fully recovered from your injuries?"

He nodded. London had hoped the change of subject would get him talking about something other than her. She wanted to ask more questions about the accident. Mason hadn't given anyone much more information than that they had stumbled upon a bomb.

Still standing across from each other, London had no idea what he was thinking, but his stare was a little unnerving.

"What?"

"The other day you ran into the club as if someone was chasing you. Was it Cory?"

"Nah, I'm still a little paranoid. It felt like someone was watching me, but I didn't see anyone. Cory had me so freaked out by the time I left Charlotte, so I'm sure it's going to take a while for me to get back to normal. He doesn't even know I'm here."

"Are you sure?"

London hoped she was overreacting regarding Cory. Why would he go through the trouble of hunting her down in another state?

"I'm pretty sure."

CHAPTER FOUR

The next day, Mason stood with his arm around London's shoulder. They were at her parents' and grandparents' gravesites looking at the headstones lined up side-by-side.

"Are you cold?" he asked when she shivered. As he placed a kiss against her temple, flashbacks of the day before invaded his mind.

All night Mason had thought about the kiss they'd shared in Harper's kitchen, as well as the conversation about London's ex-boyfriend. Mason wasn't sure what nagged him the most—the fact that a man had put his hands on her in anger, or the fact that Mason had enjoyed the kiss even more than before. He wasn't sure what to make of the strong feelings he was having. She had always meant the world to him, but now …

"I'm okay. I am a little surprised that it's this chilly out here. Usually spring in Atlanta is a little warmer. I can't ever remember it being this cold this time of year. But today, the temperature barely made it … I'm rambling,"

London sobbed, dabbing at her eyes again with the crumbled tissue in her hand. "Maybe we should leave."

"You sure? I'm in no hurry."

Her watery gaze lifted to his and it was as if a fist wrapped around his heart and squeezed. The horrible things he'd witnessed in Afghanistan would haunt him until the day he died, but nothing cut through his soul like seeing tears in her eyes.

"Thank you. Thank you so much for coming with me."

He caressed her soft cheek with the back of his hand. "Anytime. There's no other place I'd rather be." And he meant it. The more time they spent together, the more he wanted to be with her. His brain sent alerts, warning him to keep his distance, especially knowing how strong of an attraction they had for each other. But the other part of him wanted to spend as much time with her as possible and get to know the woman she had become. She was no longer Tiny, his other sister, but she was a stunning and very desirable woman. That's the part that scared the hell out of him.

London stepped out of his hold and placed the last rose on her mother's headstone before returning to him. "When I die, I don't want to be buried. I either want my body donated to science or cremated. I don't want you guys visiting me at some cold, dreary cemetery."

She stared up at him and he stood dumbfounded. How was he supposed to respond to something like that?

"Okay?"

"Uh," he fought for the right words, "can we not talk about that right now?"

Her shoulder's sagged. "All right."

Mason had sidestepped the conversation, but he had a feeling the subject would come back up. The military had prepared him for death, but so help him, he didn't want to think about losing any member of his family, especially London.

They headed back to his Cadillac Escalade, his arms draped around her shoulders again. She had planned to go to the cemetery by herself until he insisted on joining her. Now he was really glad he had.

"Why don't we go and get some lunch?" Mason suggested, helping her into the truck.

"I'm not really hungry," she said when he climbed in on the driver's side. "I just want to go home, or back to Harper's place I should say."

"You need to eat, Tiny." Lately she was never hungry. He'd seen the time when she could eat a large pizza by herself. Yet the other day she'd barely eaten two slices. "Besides, I'm kind of enjoying your company."

"So do you plan to force feed me or something? Because I'm serious, Mase, I'm not hungry."

"Well then you can watch me eat."

That got a smile out of her and it was like witnessing a sunrise. "Okay, but as long as it's not a buffet. I will never go to an all-you-can-eat joint with you ever again."

Mason laughed remembering the time he had insisted on her and his siblings going to a buffet during one of his rare visits home. None of them were big fans of the establishment, especially Cameron, who could whip up a gourmet meal with his eyes closed. Yet, they agreed—probably out of guilt since he was only in town for a few days—and had made a big deal about them spending time together. By the time they walked out of the place, four hours later, they were all saying that they would never again sit in a restaurant that long again.

"I have never in my life met a man who can put away food like you."

"That was a long time ago. I don't eat like that anymore." Now that he was getting older, he was more conscientious about what he ate. "Okay, we won't go to an all-you-can-eat place. I have another idea."

"Oh boy," she moaned.

Mason divided his attention between the road and London. He had to do something to cheer her up. He guided his truck toward Midtown. One of his friends told him about *Top Golf*, a place where they could hit a few golf balls, listen to music and eat. According to the guy, it was a cross between a bowling alley and a nightclub, only you got to hit golf balls.

"Have you ever golfed?"

Turning to him, London frowned. "Does miniature golf count?"

Mason chuckled. "Nah, that doesn't really count. Although that is a good way to work on your short game."

"Short game?"

"Putting," he explained. "I'm thinking we'll check out this new spot where we can hit a few golf balls and eat."

"Masonnnn." She dragged out his name, exasperation dripping from the two syllables.

"Come on, Tiny. Spend the rest of the day with me. You know you want to." He wiggled his eyebrows and grinned.

She laughed and the sound warmed him. "Fine. But if I accidently hit you with the golf club don't say I didn't warn you."

Now he was the one laughing. "I'll take my chances."

A short while later, Mason stood behind London, his hands over hers as he explained the proper way to grip the club.

"Try to relax and drop your left shoulder," he said close to her ear, her familiar fragrance enticing all of his senses. Suddenly standing behind her, with her butt rubbing up against the front of his body, wasn't his best idea. He felt like a jerk since all he wanted to do at the moment was grind against her backside and kiss her scented neck.

"This is too hard," she grumbled.

Heck, he was too hard. And getting harder by the minute each time she moved her sweet little ass against him.

"We have all afternoon. You'll get it. As you swing the club back, keep your left arm straight and your attention on the ball."

"How am I supposed to do all of that at the same time, especially with you breathing down my neck … literally?"

Mason burst out laughing and straightened. "You know what? Just hit the damn ball." He backed farther away when she glared at him playfully and held the club as if planning to hit him.

For the next hour they laughed, swung at golf balls, and munched on chicken wings and cheese fries. It was good to see her smiling again. If only for a little while, Mason had done what he set out to do: make her forget about her problems. He could help her get acclimated to the city and help her find a place to live. Unfortunately, he hadn't figured out what to do about her jerk of an ex-boyfriend.

*

Days later, London stood outside of Mason's door even though it was ajar. He had buzzed her up to his loft minutes ago, but she hadn't ventured inside.

This is a bad idea.

She had called earlier to see if he would be home, telling him she wanted to stop by for a little while. He hadn't asked why, but told her he would be home all evening.

London's gaze jerked up when the door eased open. Mason stood in the doorway with his cell phone to his ear and a frown on his face. He looked so good in a fitted Hawk's T-shirt that stretched across his chest and hugged his thick biceps.

"Wiz, hold on a second." Mason lowered the phone to the side of his jeans, covering the mouthpiece. "What's wrong? Why are you still standing out here?"

"I … I didn't want to just walk in."

He studied her for a moment, his gaze meeting hers as if searching for something in her eyes. Without a word, he reached for her hand and pulled her inside, closing the door behind her.

"Make yourself comfortable. I'll be off the phone in a second." He strolled into the kitchen and resumed his conversation.

London roamed around the loft, taking in the exposed brick and duct work that gave the space an industrial feel. The wall of windows, the focal point of the living space, drew her to them. There were no pictures on the walls and the floors were bare of any rugs. She moved around the huge, brown leather furniture—which was so Mason—and smiled. Harper had been trying to get him to let her decorate the space, but he wasn't having it. Mason liked comfortable and simple. His sister didn't do simple.

London peered out the window, taking in the park across the street. She had an important question to ask Mason and she had no idea how he would respond.

"Yeah, I'd appreciate that. You can just email me the information," she heard Mason say before disconnecting his call.

"Have you eaten?" he asked from across the room.

London glanced over her shoulder. "Are you going to ask me that every time you see me?"

"Yes." He set a plate in the microwave and London turned back to the window.

Seconds later the microwave beeped. The smell of something sweet and tangy permeated the air and London groaned. It was as if the delicious scent had some type of power over her, pulling her back toward the kitchen.

"That smells amazing." She sat at the breakfast bar and Mason slid the plate closer to her.

"Glad you think so. I'm sure Cam will be glad to hear that, but maybe you should taste it first."

Spearing a meatball, London dipped it into the buttery mashed potatoes. "Are you kidding me? Everything he makes is scrumptious."

Mason placed a glass of wine next to London and a beer on the counter for himself. He sat on the stool next to her, a mound of food covering his plate.

"I don't know where you put all of the food you eat."

"Like you, I have a fast metabolism. Unlike you, I don't forget to eat."

"I eat." Her words lacked conviction. He was right. For the last few weeks, eating had been the last thing on her mind.

They ate and, as usual, small talk flowed easily between them. This was what she missed living alone in North Carolina. Even when she and Cory were together, dinnertime wasn't comfortable. He constantly complained about work or his family. But with Mason, conversation was different. Their topics ranged from entertainment news to real estate, and everything in between.

"Thanks again for going to the cemetery with me the other day." London wiped her mouth with the napkin he'd handed her. "I knew I wanted to go and visit them, but it wasn't something I was looking forward to."

Mason leaned over and bumped her shoulder with his. "Anytime, baby. I'm here for you. You know that." He always said the right thing, making her love him that much more.

Mason turned slightly to face her. "Although you're always welcomed here, what sparked this visit?"

With her elbows on the counter, London toyed with the napkin in her hand. She had never been shy about going after what she wanted, but this time was different. Her heart and self-respect were on the line.

"I have a proposition for you," she blurted.

Mason's left brow rose. "Okay." He stretched out the word. Taking a swig of his beer, he waited for her to say more.

"I want to have your baby."

*

Beer spewed out of Mason's mouth and he slammed the bottle down on the countertop.

"Wh-what?" he sputtered, wiping his chin with the back of his hand. He grabbed a few napkins and cleaned up the wet mess. "What the hell are you talking about?"

He hovered over her, one hand on the counter and the other on the back of her barstool. Clearly he had heard her wrong. The London he knew wouldn't make an offer like that to anyone. Not even him.

She stood and walked into the living room, effectively putting space between them. She didn't sit; instead, she paced in front of the sofa. Mason had a feeling he was the one who needed to sit down for this conversation. He reclaimed his seat at the breakfast bar, spinning the stool in order to face her.

"I was thinking," she started, still moving and not looking at him, "I'm ready to start a family and since you want children, I figured—"

"Wait." Mason eased out of his seat trying to control the sudden tension gripping his shoulders. "The *only* way you could know that I'm ready to have children is if Harper said something to you. And I know you guys weren't sitting around talking about my personal business."

London glanced at him, her bottom lip twisted between her teeth. She looked so damn cute when she did that, but right now he was ready to wring her neck as well as his sister's.

Mason shook his head, still trying to make sense of her *proposition*. He felt as if he was in a race and everyone was suddenly ten paces ahead of him and he hadn't seen them pass. What could she be thinking? He wanted to ask, but didn't know if he was prepared for the answer. He'd be lying if he said that since London's return to Atlanta, not a day had gone by that he hadn't thought about her.

Guilt boiled in his gut. Unfortunately, his thoughts had bordered on X-rated. Definitely not the brotherly behavior he used to have where she was concerned. From day one, when they were ten years old, there was a powerful pull he felt whenever she was near. Today he couldn't explain it no more than he could back then. But this ...

"Let me get this straight. You want to have my baby." He folded his arms, noting her discomfort as she paced. She stopped to glance at him, and then started pacing again. "Did my sister happen to tell you the part of our conversation when I told her that I had no intention of getting married?"

"Yes." London stopped moving. "She told me, but I don't care. I've thought about this long and hard. I want you to be the father of my children. I don't need to be a wife to become a mother."

Mason's mouth dropped open. "You can't be serious, Tiny. You've always wanted to get married and have a family. Even I know that. That's all you and Harper talked about growing up. Why the change?"

"Because I want *you* to be the father of my children. Whenever I have talked about marriage, it's been with you in mind. But since you don't want to get married, I'll just settle for having your children."

Mason released a humorless laugh as he approached her. His heart hammered an erratic beat as he tried to process what she was saying. *Where the heck is all of this coming from?* To say he was shocked by her revelation would be an understatement. There's no way she was prepared to give up her dream of marriage. And though he knew enough people with strong marriages, that wasn't the path he wanted to take. He lived a simple, comfortable life with no drama. He already knew that when a woman was added to that equation, drama followed.

"London, you don't have to settle for anything. You're an intelligent, gorgeous, and remarkable woman. Any man would be lucky to have you."

"But there's only one man I want." The words were spoken so quietly, Mason barely heard her before she sat on the sofa.

Sighing, he rubbed his head. He'd taken out targets in Afghanistan from a hundred yards out and survived several tours oversees, yet he was way out of his element with the route this conversation was going.

He sat next to London and gathered her in his arms. The same electrical spark that always consumed him whenever he touched her was stronger than ever, but he tried to ignore it. He had to figure out how to talk some sense into her.

"Where is all of this coming from?" His lips grazed her temple as she snuggled closer. "Why now? Why proposition me now?" What had Cory done to her to make her settle for less than what she wanted?

He planned to find out everything he could about Cory. Mason's friend, Wiz, a former Navy SEAL who was now a private investigator and part owner of a security firm in Chicago, was digging into Cory's life. A computer genius, Wiz would no doubt find information about Cory that his own mother didn't know.

London released a weighted sigh. "I want a family of my own. I'm thirty-three years old and I'm not getting any younger. My window of opportunity to have safe pregnancies and healthy babies is closing. Besides that, I'm tired of dating."

"Don't let your experience with one jerk stop you from seeking the type of relationship you want. There are some great guys out there." Mason couldn't believe he was encouraging her to seek out other men. He already knew he would hate all of them because none of them would be good enough for her. Yet, despite those feelings, he couldn't be that man. Besides, it would be too weird for them to cross that family/friend line.

"It's not just one experience. I've dated and …"

"And what?"

"And none of them have been you. Everyone I have dated, I've compared to you and they don't come close to the man you are."

A smile tugged at the corner of Mason's lips. "Of course they don't. You're never going to find anyone as amazing as me."

She jabbed him in the ribs with her pointy elbow.

"Ow." He held on to her when she tried pulling away. "Seriously, though. You need to aim higher. I have enough flaws that will send you running for the hills."

"You forget," she glanced up at him, "I know your flaws. But I also know your strengths. I know you're fun to be around, dependable, trustworthy, a perfect gentleman, you believe in God, you're brave, and fiercely protective of those you love. And that's just to name a few of your qualities. Qualities that I'm looking for in the father of my children."

Mason sat speechless. He'd never been a big conversationalist, often preferring to be alone. So having this discussion, with London of all people, was mind blowing.

She pushed against his side, bringing his attention back to the present. "Does your hesitation have anything to do with you thinking that I'm not good enough for you?"

Mason frowned. "Of course not! Why would you even say something like that?"

"Because besides that kiss a couple of years ago and the one the other day, you've never made a move on me. Actually, in those two instances, you didn't make the first move. I did. What else am I supposed to think?" She stood, but he reached out for her arm, halting her.

"First of all, you would slap my face if you knew how attracted to you I am and how often I've imagined you in some compromising positions … with me. The reason I haven't made a move on you is because I have always looked at you as a little sister, a member of our family."

"But I'm not your sister, Mason!" She jerked her arm out of his grasp. "It pisses me off every time you say that. The way you kissed me back the other day was proof that there's something more … something special between us. Something passionate and hot. I'm willing and ready to see what that is. What about you?"

"I'm not looking for a wife."

"I didn't ask you to be my husband. I asked you to be the father of my children."

Alrighty then. I guess she told me.

Mason didn't have a comeback. Hell, he didn't know what to think. She was definitely the type of woman he could see as a mother for his children, but could he leave it at that? Could he father children with her without his heart screwing everything up? He doubted it, yet he couldn't help but wonder, *What if?*

CHAPTER FIVE

Days after propositioning Mason, London made up the bed in Harper's guest bedroom thinking that maybe she hadn't done the right thing. Part of her wondered what she'd been thinking. Whereas the other part of her was glad she had presented him with the idea. Her rationale was that all he could say was no.

He hadn't said no. At least not completely.

London organized the satin pillows on top of the comforter, thankful that Harper didn't mind sharing her space. For the past three weeks, they had co-existed as if they'd lived together forever. London was not only grateful for the roof over her head, but also for Harper's company. The longer she was in Charlotte, the lonelier she had gotten. When Harper suggested she move back home to Atlanta, London used it as a sign. She had already been considering returning, and Harper's words and the news anchor position that had opened up were just the encouragement she needed.

"Hey," London roamed into the kitchen, "I'm surprised you're here. I thought you were spending the night with your new man." She smiled, genuinely happy for her friend. Harper's new beau, Hunter, didn't live in Atlanta, but was in town for a few months on business. London had a feeling things were getting pretty serious between them.

"Yeah, he had an early morning meeting so we cut the night short." Harper poured her and London a cup of coffee. Croissants and fruit sat in the center of the dining room table, and a pitcher of orange juice completed the continental breakfast.

"Well, if you ever decide you want to bring him home, just let me know and I'll make myself scarce." London's mouth watered as she reached for a croissant. When she first arrived back in Atlanta, she had to remind herself to eat. Now her appetite had come back with a vengeance. "You must have been awake for a while. This all looks delicious. I didn't even hear you bumping around."

"Good. I was trying to be quiet so that you could get some sleep. I don't know how you do it. Getting up at two o'clock in the morning to get ready for work and then not getting home until after seven some days, is crazy."

"This schedule has been taking some getting used to." Once she got acclimated to her work hours and new co-workers, she had no doubt life would get a little easier. She didn't know what she would do if she didn't have one weekday as well as the weekends off. Any free time she spent with Mason gave her even more reasons to look forward to not being at work. She loved how he always made himself available to her, but she had a feeling a big part of that was so he could keep an eye on her.

Harper lifted her juice glass. "I have an event at the club later on tonight. What do you have going on today?"

"Besides doing laundry, grocery shopping, and going to the gym? Not too much." London bit into the croissant. "There's something I wanted to talk to you about."

Harper eyed her over her juice glass. "Sounds serious."

London finished chewing. The flaky treat suddenly landed hard in her stomach as trepidation swirled in her gut.

"I propositioned your brother last night." She braced herself for Harper's outburst. Their conversation weeks ago about how Mason wanted children, but not a wife, had been playing around in her head constantly.

"Well, it's about time you went after your man." Harper spooned up a bowl of fruit for each of them and handed one to London. "I'm surprised it took you this long. With all the time you two have been spending with each other, I figured at least one of you would come to your senses. I'm sure a little seduction is all you need to reel my brother in."

"Wow, I'm surprised you're okay with this. I thought for sure you'd read me the riot act."

"Of course I'm okay with you two getting together. I've been trying to play match-maker for you and Mason for most of our lives."

"I know, but you're going easy on me. I thought for sure you'd give me a hard time like you gave him about wanting kids without a spouse."

Harper's fork stopped midair. "Hold up. Wait! What are you talking about?" Harper's frown slowly turned into a scowl as realization must have dawned on her and she narrowed her eyes.

"Before you—"

"Surely you haven't done what I think you've done. No way are you thinking about going along with his nonsense! Have you lost your mind?"

"Oh here we go." London sighed loudly, plopping a small piece of cantaloupe into her mouth. "I should have known you didn't understand what I was saying."

"You're right, I don't understand. Why would you even consider something so crazy? What happened to you wanting a family? Which includes a husband I might add. I didn't tell you about the conversation with him for you to go half-cocked and throw yourself at him like this."

"You, better than anyone, know how much Mason means to me. I'm in love with him, Harp. My decision to have children with him is a no brainer. We get along great and I can't think of anyone I would want to co-parent with other than him. Besides, he would make an amazing father."

"He'll make an amazing husband, too, but you're thinking about letting him off the hook from that role. I know you and Mason love each other … I've known it for years. Don't give him an out. Make his butt commit to the *whole* family dynamic! Not just to having children. That's the problem with so many women today. These men get to have the fun of making a baby, without all of the responsibility that goes along with it."

"You know as well as I do that Mason would be a full-time dad."

"I know, but you want a family. Not just a baby daddy! I am not going to let you settle."

London lunged out of her chair, her arms around her midsection. "You just don't get it, Harp."

"Get what? What am I not getting? All I know is that you're willing to—"

"Did you know that I'm the same age as my mother was when she was killed?" London huffed out a breath. "She was taken from me before she could even tell me about what to expect when I started my period. We didn't get a chance to have that mother/daughter talk about boys and dating. I can barely remember mother/daughter shopping trips or going to get our nails done. Unlike you, and most of the people I know, most of my life was spent without my parents. I'm sick of being alone! I'm ready to have my own family." Emotion clogged London's throat and her body tensed trying to keep herself from falling apart.

"London, don't do this to yourself," Harper whispered, concern filling her eyes.

"My grandparents stepped in for my parents, but it wasn't the same. They were already up in age. All they could really do for me was clothe and provide me with a roof over my head."

Her heart squeezed in her chest. She was so grateful for her grandparents. At least she didn't end up in foster care. But she knew how much she missed out on.

"If it weren't for Cameron, who helped me with my homework, or Mason, my guardian angel, and you … God, Harper, I don't know what I would have done without you."

"Girl, you're going to make me cry." Harper hugged her tight, sniffling. "You're my sister. I can't imagine my life without you either. That's why I want the best for you. I love my brother more than life, but that idea about having children out of wedlock … intentionally, is a horrible idea."

"Maybe so." London straightened, and blew out a breath, pulling out of Harper's hold. "But he and I want the same thing."

"No you don't. How can you say that? You want the whole family unit and Mason only wants children. Two very different things."

"Okay, so it's a bad idea, but it's an idea that I'm considering in order to have children with a man I love. Who knows, maybe at some point he'll consider marrying me."

"Do you hear yourself? What makes you think you'll be able to change a man, especially my stubborn brother? Many women have tried and failed. If Mason's mind is set on having children and nothing else, chances are, that's all he's going to want. Are you prepared for that?"

No. London knew she wouldn't be able to handle being rejected by Mason.

"What am I supposed to do, Harper? I don't want to live my life alone anymore. Yes, I want a husband and children who I can build a home with, but what if no one ever comes along? I'm not getting any younger. I don't want to be too old to chase after my babies." Sighing, she rubbed her forehead, the fight gone out of her. "Mason is a perfect choice, because I don't want to have a baby with someone I don't love."

Harper hesitated before speaking. "What did Mason say about all of this?"

"First he freaked out a little. His reaction was similar to yours. But once we talked, he really didn't say much one way or the other."

"Hmm, so he didn't shoot the idea down," Harper said as if talking to herself. "Well, if Mason is the right man for you, he'll recognize it sooner or later ... hopefully."

"He is the right man for me." London just had to show him.

*

Standing in the middle of his brother's living room, Mason tapped his cell phone against his chin. He had just finished a call to London, inviting her over to his place later that evening. It was time they discussed her proposition—the one she'd made three days ago.

He had talked with Wiz, and learned that Cory was at work in Charlotte on London's first day back in Atlanta. Wiz had also sent him a ton of information about Cory including work history, bank records, and a police record, as well as a recent photo. Besides what London said took place while in North Carolina the last few months, Cory didn't appear to be a threat. But Mason had every intention of keeping his eyes and ears opened.

He walked back into the kitchen and leaned on the counter.

Cameron set a bag on the countertop next to Mason and started placing covered dishes filled with food inside of it. "Problems?"

"No. Just thinking."

"About?"

"About London. About that chump, Cory. And just stuff."

"Sounds like you were able to get some info about the chump."

"Yep, Wiz came through. He sent me background info yesterday and faxed me some additional stuff earlier today, including the dude's photo."

"That's good. Give me a copy of his picture so that I can keep an eye out for him."

"Will do."

"How's London doing?"

"She's all right. She hasn't said anything more about Cory. Except, she asked me to promise her that I wouldn't do anything to him."

Cameron chuckled. "And what did you say?"

"As long as the guy stays away from her, he won't have any problems from me. But let him show up. His ass is mine."

Cameron loaded the last dish into the bag before saying, "I see. Well, on another note, you need to learn how to cook. I'm not going to keep hooking you up with meals so that you can snag a woman. Even if it is London." His brother had a sharp business mind, but his cooking abilities were second to none.

"Who says I'm trying to snag a woman, especially London?" Mason wondered what Cameron had heard.

"Are you saying that you're not interested in her? Weren't you just talking to her on the telephone? Why ask her to meet you at your place tonight if you're not interested?"

Instead of telling his brother about London's proposition, Mason said, "Because I'm worried about her."

"I'm worried about London, too. However, I haven't been daydreaming about her or hanging out with her every chance I get. I call and check on her like I would Harp, but you—"

Cameron stopped when the cordless telephone sitting on the counter rang. Snatching the phone, Mason glanced at the screen before his brother could get to it. "Ahh, Simone. No wonder you're all up in my personal life. You've found love and feel that everyone else should, too, huh?"

"Give me the damn phone." Cameron grabbed the device. A smile spread across his face as he moved out of the kitchen to speak with Simone. Minutes later, he returned and set the phone back on the counter.

"That was quick."

"She was just confirming our plans for the evening."

"Oh. Well, just so that we're clear, I'm not trying to snag anyone." Mason sat at the round kitchen table. He had a few minutes before he had to head home. "I'm making sure London eats."

"Yeah right. Tell it to someone who doesn't know you. The two of you have been dancing around each other for most of your adult lives."

"I've been overseas for most of my adult life. So—"

"Doesn't matter. She's the one who makes your heart beat faster. The one who causes you frustrated and sleepless nights. She's the one—"

"What the hell, man? Simone's got your nose so wide open you think everyone is madly in love?"

Cameron chuckled, not denying anything. "I'm just saying that when the right woman comes along, you can't let her go. Granted, I know you have this hang up about being in a serious relationship, but get over it. You need to go ahead and claim London before someone else does."

Mason's pulse kicked up. He pulled a pina colada sucker from his pocket, unwrapped it, and shoved it into his mouth. He'd been trying to break the habit of indulging in the gourmet lollipops, but they had been a source of comfort since returning to the States. As for London, sure he wanted her to be happy, even if it meant her being with someone else. But the thought of her with another man made him crazy. He struggled to ignore her tempting proposal. Was he ready to cross that line and be more than friends?

"I'll take your silence as an 'I'm in love with her and I don't know what the hell to do about it'."

Mason removed the lollipop from his mouth. "It's not that simple, Cam, and you know it."

"Everything is only as hard as you make it."

"Man, she's like our sis—"

"Quit lying. You wouldn't want to screw your sister. And don't insult my intelligence and tell me it's not like that. You want her. I could tell years ago. Even more so when all of us were at Harp's house yesterday. You two kept stealing looks at each other as if you were sharing a secret." Cameron headed up the stairs to his bedroom. "Keep dancing around her if you want. Eventually someone else will step in and take the choice from you. Lock up when you leave. I have to get ready for *my* woman."

Two hours later, Mason sat at his dining room table across from London, trying to figure out how to bring up the subject of possibly fathering her children. His brother's words rattled around in his head. Cameron was right. It was time Mason stopped kidding himself. He had never cared about a woman as much as he did London. Why not take a chance?

"Why are you staring at me like that?" London asked, her fork inches from her mouth. "You've been acting stranger than usual since I arrived."

Mason smiled. They were comfortable enough with each other to say whatever the heck they wanted. Yet another reason to see what dating her would be like.

He shook his head. He couldn't believe he was thinking about trying out a relationship again. Clearly he hadn't learned his lesson after dealing with Faith.

"Mason?"

"I've been thinking about your proposition and I have a proposition for you."

London set her fork down, her gaze steady on him. "Oh-kay. What is it?"

Instead of responding, Mason slid his chair back and moved around the small glass table. He stretched out his hand and she just stared at it before setting her smaller hand within his.

Mason pulled her against his body and cupped her face, his thumbs caressing her soft cheeks. There was something he needed to do before presenting his proposal. Something he had wanted to do from the moment she walked in.

He stared down at her. First at her eyes and then at her tempting mouth. Lowering his head, he touched his lips to hers, nipping at her top lip and then her lower one. Coaxing her lips apart with his tongue, he dived in, exploring the inner recesses of her mouth. Her sweetness poured through the kiss, sending an erotic jolt to his shaft, making Mason want more. So much more.

How could he have denied himself of the pleasure of having her in his arms again, his tongue tangling with hers? As expected, the desire sweeping through him confirmed the decision he'd made on the way home from Cameron's place.

With one last peck, Mason raised his head but kept his hands on her face. "I propose we put your proposal on the back burner."

"Ma—"

"And spend some time getting to know each other on a different level."

Her perfectly arched eyebrows dipped. "What do you mean on a different level?"

Grabbing one of her hands, he pulled her over to the sofa. "Have a seat." He sat close to her and placed his arm behind her on the back of the sofa.

"So what's this different level?"

Mason thought about what he wanted to say, trying to choose his words carefully. "You want marriage and children. I don't want you to settle for less than that."

"Mason, I'm a grown woman. I know what I want. Yes, I would love to get married and have children, but that doesn't look as if it's going to happen for me. My proposal to have children with you is a win-win."

"For me, yeah, but not for you."

"What are you talking about? I know what I'm asking of you."

"But, baby, you're willing to settle. You think you can handle being *just* my baby's mama, but I know that will never be enough for you."

She jumped up from the sofa. "I know myself better than you do, Mason! I know what I can handle and what I can't. You've been gone like … forever. You don't know what I want and what I don't want."

"All the more reason why we should spend some time getting to know each other on a deeper level. Let's not talk kids right now. Let's do things together, not like brother and sister. Go on dates. Get to know each other as man and woman."

She chuckled. "That last part sounds kinda funny."

"I know, but you know what I mean." He couldn't believe he was proposing dating anyone, especially London. But Cameron's words kept circling in Mason's head. *Eventually someone else will step in and take the choice from you.*

Despite how good she tasted and how much he cared for her, more than anything, Mason wanted what was best for London. He knew she had feelings for him, and he cared deeply for her. He just hoped he didn't hurt her.

"So are we talking dating exclusively?" London asked.

Rising, Mason approached her. "Is that going to be a problem?"

"Not for me," she quickly said.

"Me either." His gaze lingered on her lips. Mason had a feeling kissing her was about to become his favorite past time. He pulled London close, relishing the feel of her soft body against his. "There is one condition."

London hesitated, her wary gaze holding his. "And that is?"

"If at any point this arrangement doesn't work for either of us, we have to agree to talk about it. My biggest concern is that this will screw up our current relationship."

"That's not going to happen." As London ran her fingers slowly up his chest, heat crept through his body. "We've always been able to talk to each other about anything."

"That was a long time ago, Tiny. We're both very different people now." At least he knew he was. His time overseas had changed him in many ways—some good, some bad—and he had seen and experienced situations he could never wipe from his mind.

"You're right. We are different people and I can't wait to get to know the new Mason Bennett."

Grinning, he lowered his head. "And I can't wait to get to know you, Tiny."

*

London surrendered completely when Mason devoured her mouth, the flooding of uncontrollable joy consuming her body as her arms circled his neck. She pulled him closer. This was what she wanted. He was what she'd wanted and needed all along.

Even in London's most vivid dreams she hadn't expected that she and Mason would date. She had hoped and even fantasized about a relationship with him that wasn't brotherly, but she never thought those moments would come to fruition. And this—the delicious, sexy mouth devouring hers—she could get used to.

When the kiss ended, they were both breathing hard. London's hand slid down his chest and a thrill shot through her when his muscles twitched under her touch.

I'm dating Mason. The thought sent another wave of excitement from her head to the soles of her feet. The moment felt like being asked to attend prom with the captain of the football team.

"This is going to be fun," London said, her voice sexier than usual even to her own ears.

Mason chuckled and dipped his head, nipping at her neck.

Goosebumps crawled along her arms when his lips inched up and made contact with the sensitive spot behind her ear. An involuntary moan slipped out and her eyes slid closed. She gripped the front of his shirt to keep from puddling to the floor.

"I'd better stop while I can," Mason murmured against her skin before he slowly lifted his head. "I can already tell that keeping my mouth and hands off of you is going to be nearly impossible."

London grinned, feeling happier than she'd felt in a long time. "I'm counting on that."

He flashed a smile that melted her heart as they returned to the sofa. London sat so close to him ... a little bit more she'd be sitting on his lap.

"So that I'm clear, is this relation— I mean dating that we're doing, is it like friends with benefits?" London asked.

Mason shook his head. "Not friends with benefits. That wasn't the intent with my proposition. I was serious about us spending time getting to know each other. I already know you on a moral level, your likes and dislikes, now I'm looking forward to knowing everything else about you. I'm going into this setup, or should I say relationship, with my eyes wide open."

"Really?"

"Really."

"So why now? Harper said that you were against committed relationships. What's that all about?"

Mason leaned forward, his hands clasped together. "I've had two serious relationships, or at least what I'd consider serious, and they both ended badly. The first one was right after high school, before I joined the military. The woman was so insecure that she kept accusing me of cheating."

"Were you?" London looked at him pointedly, remembering when he had asked her the same question.

"Never. And I never will. I would just walk away before doing something like that to any woman. My last relationship was an off and on one. It was short and made me realize that I don't have any tolerance for stupid shit and drama. She liked to argue. I don't. It was always some issue with her. So I decided that I didn't want or need anything serious with a woman."

"So why proposition me?"

"Because you're special and I care about you. And because, according to you, we want the same thing. I want us both to see how or if we can get along well enough to even consider having and raising children together. As far as anything more than that ... I don't know what to tell you. Right now, I don't see myself married. So if you know you want more than what I'm offering, tell me now."

London said nothing. They sorta wanted the same thing. She was ready to start a family. She was willing to give up the idea of getting married in exchange for Mason fathering her children. But in her heart, she would love for them to be married first. For right now she would just see where this relationship took her.

"Okay, is there anything else I should know going into this relationship? Are there going to be women lurking in the background or coming out of the woodwork?"

"If there was someone else in my life, I wouldn't have stepped to you like this. So that's one area you definitely don't have to worry about. What about you? Besides Cory, is there anyone I need to be concerned about?"

"Nope. You don't even have to worry about Cory. He's history."

Mason said nothing and London hoped his silence didn't mean that he'd been in contact with Cory. There was no telling with Mason, but she didn't want to ruin the moment and ask. She had moved on and was looking forward to getting to know him."

"So does dating you include sex?" London blurted.

Mason chuckled. "I was right. You have changed. I'm going to have to remember that you're not the shy, little kid who used to sneak into my bed."

London smiled. "Is that a yes?"

Mason burst out laughing and leaned away from her shaking his head. He laughed for a while before he said, "It can be included, but let's play this by ear. I'm a little rusty with the whole dating scene, but I'm looking forward to some new experiences with you."

"Does this mean that you'll be willing to attend an opera or a ballet with me?"

"Oh hell no." He scooted over on the sofa, but London grabbed hold of his arm. "Tiny, I haven't changed that much."

"But you're open to new experiences, right?"

Mason narrowed his eyes at her. "*Some* new experiences."

That was good enough for London. Giddiness bubbled inside of her and she felt like a little kid in the Disney store. Dating Mason was going to be fun.

CHAPTER SIX

Despite the strobe lights, Mason saw her when she stepped into view, but then again, who could miss her? The way Faith Hanson's hips swayed from side to side in a rhythmic motion with each long stride she took, garnered attention from both men and women. A beautiful woman with flawless skin, doe-like eyes, and long, flowing hair, Faith had a body that would make any man's mouth water.

Mason felt nothing.

For the past month, he only had eyes for one woman. What he once felt for Faith was nothing compared to the way his heart raced and pulse pounded whenever London entered a room. The woman he'd known since childhood had officially snagged his heart and was starting to make him believe in a lifetime love.

Spotting him, Faith headed to the stairs that led up to the VIP section, where Mason stood. He'd been pulled in different directions all night. One of his guys had to leave because his wife went into labor and they'd had two call-ins that night. He didn't mind filling in, though. Hanging out in the club gave him a chance to see how well his security team was managing. It also gave him an opportunity to see if there were any shortcomings in the systems they had in place.

"Well, hello, handsome. It's been a long time," Faith crooned over the music, invading Mason's personal space when she attempted to kiss his lips. He leaned back in time for her kiss to catch air, but not in time to avoid the assault of her overpowering perfume.

Mason coughed, trying to catch his breath. *What the heck did she do, swim inside the perfume bottle?*

"Hello, Faith," he finally responded. "Yes, it has been a while."

"I've missed you." She batted her long eyelashes and placed her hands on his chest, her fingers inching their way up before he could stop her. Grabbing her wrists, he set her back away from him, ignoring the way her red lips pouted. "Oh, so it's like that?"

"Yeah, it is. But you knew that already since I've told you that on more than one occasion. I'm *still* not interested."

"I figured you'd change your mind once you remembered what you were missing." She ran her hands slowly down the sides of her curvaceous body, purring as she watched him watch her. The little black dress she had on was so damn tight, it was a wonder she could breathe.

"What do you want, Faith?"

She stepped closer again. "You."

"That's not gonna to happen."

He stared down at her, disgusted with himself that he'd spent any time with her in the past. She was a drama queen and as fake as the cubic zirconia stones dripping from her ears and hanging around her neck.

Now that he and London were building upon their relationship, he realized that he didn't want just companionship, but possibly a serious commitment. The thought didn't freak him out as it once had.

"Well, I guess if I can't have you, I'll have to settle for the VIP section." She stepped to the left, but Mason blocked her path to the stairs.

"Sorry. The VIP sections are off limit tonight. We have a few private parties going on."

Mason almost laughed when her sexy smile quickly turned into an angry pout. "You and your men used to always let me up there!"

"Mase, London's on her way over," Hamilton announced in Mason's earpiece.

"All right, thanks," he responded.

Ignoring Faith and her pouting, Mason glanced around until he spotted London weaving between people, heading his way. When she came into better view, his heart skipped a beat and his shaft stirred.

Damn.

Seeing her in the short, one-shoulder, red dress made him want to find a secluded spot and have his way with her.

The left corner of his mouth lifted slowly in appreciation. She was wearing the hell out that dress. Most importantly, she was all his.

Mason looked forward to seeing her every chance he got and tonight was no different. With their hectic work schedules, finding time to spend together was proving to be more challenging than he had originally thought. But he had every intention of changing that. Being part owner of the club had its advantages. He planned to adjust his schedule around hers.

After not seeing her for the last two days, he had invited her to the club when he snagged an invitation to one of her favorite actresses' birthday party. The A-lister had reserved two of the club's VIP lounges to celebrate. Mason hadn't been sure London would attend since her work day had started at three that morning, but here she was.

Faith huffed out a breath. "Mason I don't appreci—"

He tuned her out and tension descended on him like a lion on a herd of gazelles when two college-age guys stepped to London. He didn't know what they were saying, but when one of the guys, with broad shoulders, blocked his view of her, Mason almost left his post, but stopped. One by one, they handed London a slip of paper and she scribbled what he assumed was her autograph on them. There were times when Mason forgot that she was a television personality. Lately when they were out, people walked up to her asking for an autograph or acknowledging that they'd seen her on TV.

She eased around the guys, nodding and smiling at something they said. Mason hated being an overprotective jerk, but with her, he couldn't help it. She was one of the sweetest people he knew and she was so petite, he felt people tended to try and take advantage of her. Then again, she was a grown woman, capable of taking care of herself. Yet, he wanted to be the one to take care of her.

London resumed her trek toward him, but slowed when she saw Faith standing way too close to him.

"You need to back off of me, Faith," Mason said with more force than intended, but it worked. She took a step back, but there still wasn't enough space between them as far as he was concerned.

"So you gon' let me upstairs or what?" she asked, her sultry tone more irritating than seductive.

"Like I said, the VIP sections aren't available. Maybe another night."

Mason reached for London when she stood back, probably waiting for Faith to get out of the way considering she was still standing directly in front of him. He didn't know what Faith was up to, but she'd been blowing up his cell phone, not catching a hint of his disinterest. Maybe it was time for her to see one of the reasons why he no longer had an interest in her.

"Hey, baby," he greeted London when she molded her sexy body against his. She turned her angelic face up to him and smiled. "I was wondering if you were going to make it. I'm glad to see you."

"Not as glad as I am to see you." Her mouth covered his in a scorching kiss and suddenly Mason didn't give a damn about the VIP sections. He would never get tired of tasting London's sweet lips, which currently tasted of peppermint and liquor. Apparently she'd been at the club for a while if she'd had time for a drink.

Mason almost moaned when she pulled her mouth from his. "Well, hello to you, too."

"Hi." She stared up at him, a twinkle in her eyes and a smile on her delicious lips. "Have you missed me?"

"You know I have."

"Ahem," Faith cleared her throat. "I guess I know why you haven't returned my calls. You're sampling a new flavor this month."

Mason stared down at London, his arm around her waist, his hand resting possessively on her hip. "Nah, Faith, she's more than a flavor of the month."

"Really?" Disdain dripped from the one word as she looked London up and down, turning up her pert nose.

"So you're telling me that you gave up all of this, for … for her?"

"Yeah, that's exactly what I'm telling you. Let me introduce you to my woman. London, this is Faith. Faith, London."

"Hello," London said, and Faith nodded, neither bothering with a handshake.

Faith squinted and pointed a long, manicured finger at London. "Haven't I seen you before? You look a little familiar."

"She's a news anchor on Hot Atlanta News."

"Oh yeah, that's it. I saw your face on the side of a bus."

Neither Mason or London said anything, but again Mason questioned his choice of past women in his life. It was good he cut her loose when he had.

"I guess I'll see you around, Mase." Faith squeezed his arm. The seductive smile was probably meant to entice, but only disgusted him since she was clearly disrespecting London. "Give me a call sometime. Maybe we can pick up where we left off since I'm sure you'll soon realize what you're missing." She sauntered away, an extra swing in her hips.

London waited a moment before saying, "You sure know how to pick 'em."

He chuckled, glad she wasn't one of those women to fly off the handle seeing her man talking to another woman. "And you sure know how to make an entrance. Walking in here looking like every man's fantasy. You look hot, baby."

"Thank you. I wore this little number for you."

"In that case, I should be the one to take it off of you." He placed a lingering kiss against her temple and moved closer to her ear. "You should come home with

79

me tonight. That dress has me imagining all the wicked things I want to do to you."

"Mmm, sounds enticing and I don't have to work tomorrow."

"Even better."

*

Hours later, Mason carried London into his loft, pushing the door closed with his foot. She held on tight, her arms around his neck, her strappy, red sandals dangling from her fingers. All night she kept thinking about how they were about to take their relationship to the next level.

"You can put me down now." Her feet had been aching while at the club, and the moment she climbed into Mason's truck, she slipped off her shoes. Once they arrived at his place, she started to put them back on, but he stopped her by lifting her out of the truck. He had yet to put her down. "Mase, I don't expect you to carry me all the way upstairs."

Without responding, he turned slightly and flipped a switch that casted a dim light near the stairs. London loved his loft. It was simply decorated, but it had some of the coolest features like blinds that were operated by a remote control, and stairs that lit up when stepped on.

Once they were up the stairs, Mason headed to the master bedroom. The moment they strolled across the threshold, the scent of sandalwood and citrus permeated the air. The bedroom, large with a huge bed in the center of the room, smelled like Mason.

London yawned the moment he set her on her feet near the bed. At two-thirty in the morning, she had been up twenty-four hours and exhaustion was setting in. Yet, she wasn't tired enough to forego a night that she'd fantasized about on more than one occasion.

Mason turned on the small lamp on the bedside table, which dimly lit the room. He removed his gun holster, setting the gun in the top drawer of the table and placing the holster on a nearby hook.

London watched as he quickly went through his routine before going back to the hall and turning off the light. Suddenly the room was even more romantic. She had been in his bedroom before tonight, but they had only slept together. No sex. They had come to an agreement to focus on getting to know each other before adding sex to the equation.

Tonight would be different. A quiver raked over her flesh. They were really going to do this.

She remained next to the bed as Mason tossed his suit jacket across the lone chair near the window and loosened his tie before discarding it into the chair as well. All the while, his gaze remained on her. Sometimes his intense eyes held so much mystery, but tonight all she saw was desire … and love.

"Come here," he said. He turned on the small speaker that held his iPod. The sexy sounds of R&B singer, Leigh Bush, filled the room. "I didn't get a chance to dance with you tonight."

London's brows shot up. "And you want to do that *now?*"

A crooked grin spread across his mouth. "Yes, now."

London ambled across the room, the hardwood floor cool beneath her bare feet. She was six or seven inches shorter than Mason when she wasn't in her heels, so this was going to be interesting.

He pulled her into his arms. With one of her hands within his, she looped her free arm around his waist and laid her head against his chest. The steady beat of his heart along with the lyrics from "A Night in Forever" washed over her like an intimate caress. She had heard the song before, but tonight the words seemed so fitting to where she and Mason were in their relationship, and where they were in that moment.

Their bodies swayed to the smooth melody and she fell more in love with him. She never pegged him for the romantic type, but with dimmed lights, music, and dancing, she could easily get used to this side of him.

She lifted her head. "I thought you didn't like to dance."

Mason gave a slight shrug. "I wouldn't necessarily say I don't like dancing, but I'm particular about who I dance with." He spun her, which wasn't easy in her bare feet, and pulled her back to him. "And I love dancing with you."

Cradling the back of her head, he lowered his mouth to hers, still swaying to the beat of the music. He gently coaxed her lips apart, kissing her with a hunger that mirrored the lust swirling within her. Shivers of desire raced through her body, nipping at every nerve ending as his kiss grew more demanding. She wanted him. God, she wanted him more than she had ever wanted anything in her life.

As the song ended and the next one started, Mason cupped her face between his hands and stared into her eyes. Her heart squeezed at the intimacy of the moment. This big, sexy, loving man was all hers.

"Did I tell you how beautiful you looked tonight?"

"You might have mentioned it a time or two."

They stood there, staring into each other's eyes, and London wondered what he was thinking. She knew he wasn't planning to change his mind about their next steps—they both were more than ready—but she wasn't sure what to make of his hesitation.

"God, you mean so much to me." His voice was thick with emotion.

Her body tightened with desire. "I feel the same about you."

It seemed he wanted to say more and opened his mouth, but closed it just as fast. Sometimes she didn't know what to make of him, but right now was not one of those time. The love shining in his eyes was so intense, London could feel it deep in her soul. He didn't need to say anything more.

She stepped out of his hold and reached for the zipper of her dress, but Mason pulled her back to him.

"I'll take care of that for you." His voice was low and sexy, his warm breath a feather against her neck. "I've been waiting all night to get you out of this dress."

A shiver shot down her back and it wasn't because of the cool breeze that touched her skin as the zipper lowered. No, it was because of what was finally getting ready to happen. It seemed she'd waited a lifetime for this moment. Finally, she would be with the man she had loved for as long as she could remember.

Mason held her hand as she stepped out of the dress. Without releasing her, he added her dress to his clothes in the chair. His gaze raked over her body as if *really* seeing her for the first time. She had only slept over twice since they'd started dating. Each time he had insisted on her sleeping in at least a T-shirt and shorts. And each time he still complained that she was a temptation that was hard to resist.

Mason's lips curved into a grin. "I'm really feelin' the red lace."

London laughed. "I'm glad you approve." She ran her hands slowly up his torso, feeling confident in only her strapless bra and panties. "You have on too many clothes. I think we should do something about that."

"I agree." Instead of taking off the rest of his clothes, like she thought he would, he lowered his large hands to her butt and pulled her tighter against his body. His erection pressed against her belly, sending all types of wicked thoughts through her mind. She was so ready to have him naked.

But Mason would not be rushed. He squeezed and kneaded her ass, as if he were prepping dough to make bread, and her pulse pounded loudly in her ears. She was already hot and ready, her sex clenching with need. Yet, he was acting as if they had all the time in the world.

"Mase," she moaned.

"Yeah, baby?" he muttered against her neck, licking, sucking, sending her senses into overdrive as he continued the sweet torture to her body.

London gripped the front of his shirt, trying to keep herself from leaping into his arms and demanding that he take her right then and there.

"Your. Clothes. Too many," she said in short spurts, squeezing her legs together to tamp down the throbbing pulse between her thighs. She struggled with the tail of his shirt, unable to work it out of his waistband while trying to unbutton it. "Mase, help me," she whined, not caring that she sounded needy. Hell, at the moment, she was needy.

Chuckling, he placed a quick kiss on her cheek and unbuckled his belt. He took his time unzipping his slacks, and her heart fluttered in anticipation. When he lowered his pants, and then his briefs, his erection sprung to attention. Her heart pounded against her ribcage like a sledgehammer banging into concrete. She wanted to touch him. Stroke him. Feel him deep inside of her.

A magnificent warmth spread through her body. "You look hot in a suit, but man, I'm thinking I like you best in your birthday suit."

Mason chuckled as his arm went around her back. With a flick of his wrist, her bra was unfastened. She stood stock still as he slowly removed the garment and then tossed it aside, not caring where it landed. His expression grew serious as he stood before her.

London bit her bottom lip. She wasn't shy, but his heated gaze was like a blow torch heating every inch of her skin. He lingered on her bare breasts as they hung free, his already dark eyes growing darker before taking in her little lace panties.

"Damn, baby," was all he said as he continued to study her body.

London squealed when Mason suddenly swept her off her feet and carried her across the room. He yanked the covers back and set her in the middle of the bed. Now he seemed like a man on a mission. Her gaze roamed over his muscular physique while he pulled a foiled packet from the drawer. All male from his wide shoulders, to his broad chest and thick biceps, on down to his flat abs. Her gaze went lower to the wispy hair that led to his engorged shaft and she knew they wouldn't be able to take this first time slow.

*

Mason climbed onto the bed and pulled London closer. Glancing down at her enticing body had him ready to dive right in. He had waited a long time to have her like this, and didn't want to rush, but damn. How the hell was he going to take his time and please her when he felt like a horny teenager? He had hoped dancing would cool him down some, so he wouldn't end up going all He-Man on her. But if anything, it only made him more hot and bothered.

"These have to go." His words came out as a hoarse growl. He slid the skimpy panties down her smooth legs and dropped them on the floor next to the bed. *Goodness.* His penis twitched as his gaze did a slow crawl along her shapely body. Her full breasts, toned thighs, and shapely legs taunted him. As if saying, *take me, I'm all yours.* "You're breathtaking."

A shy smile lit her face. "Thank you."

Mason eased between her legs, nudging them farther apart with his knees as he now stared into lust-filled eyes. His attention went back to her body. She visibly gulped when he palmed each side of her breasts, pushing them together. He had always been a breast man and she was more than a handful—just the way he liked it. Unable to help himself, Mason buried his face between them. *Heaven.* That's what it felt like being smothered in her softness. Her scent, a mixture of baby powder and flowers, surrounded him.

Lifting his head slightly, he tweaked her nipple while swirling his tongue around the other, loving the way they instantly beaded under his touch. London squirmed beneath him; her sexy whimpers had his penis growing harder with every minute that passed. He moved to the next nipple, his mouth replacing his fingers as he continued to knead her breasts.

She rubbed her hands on the back of his head, still squirming. "Mason, please. You've teased me enough. I want you."

He wanted her just as bad and had tortured them both enough. He quickly sheathed himself as he stared down into her eyes. He had never seen her look more beautiful than she did at that moment. His heart swelled with an emotion that he'd never felt with another woman. No doubt he loved her, but what he was feeling deep in his soul was something so much more powerful than just love.

He hovered above her and she reached for him, her mouth meeting his. Her kiss was warm and sweet, yet demanding and forceful, as if challenging him to make a move. He was so up for the challenge.

He deepened the kiss and she moaned into his mouth as he braced a hand on the pillow, his free hand skimming down her taut stomach to the curve of her hips. Mason gave her a little squeeze before lifting her hip and positioning himself at her opening. He pulled his mouth from hers, their lips only inches apart. Their gazes locked and he slid inside of her sweet heat.

London gasped and he sucked in a breath as her tightness wrapped around him like a snug pair of leather gloves. Mason lowered her hip. He started moving slowly, giving her body time to adjust to him as he slid in and out of her, going deeper with each thrust.

Damn she felt good.

He cursed under his breath when she wrapped her legs around his waist and arched into him. "London, baby," he ground out when her muscles clenched. He already felt as if he were about to explode. At this rate, it would be over before they got going good.

We can take it slow next time. But right now …

Mason increased his pace, thrusting into her harder, faster, bumping against her inner walls, barely holding on. They moved together in perfect sync and he knew he would never be the same after this night.

"Mase …" London whimpered, her fingernails digging into his shoulders, her hips rocking frantically. "Mason!"

she screamed, bucking hard against him as her arms flailed at her sides. "*Oh ... my ... God, Mason!*"

She shuddered and Mason kept thrusting faster and harder until his body tightened and his heart crashed against his chest. He gritted his teeth and then howled London's name as a potent orgasm gripped him, pushing him over the edge.

Sated and gasping for air, Mason held himself above her, bracing most of his weight on his forearm. Pulling out of her, he rolled onto his back.

"Damn, girl. What the hell kind of thigh workouts have you been doing? I felt like I was being held by the jaws of a vice grip."

London laughed and coughed, still breathing hard. They laid there for the longest time, their heavy breathing mingling with the background music. After what seemed like an hour, but was probably only minutes, Mason leaned toward her.

"You okay?"

"Wonderful," she said sleepily.

He kissed her sweat-slicked forehead. "I'll be right back." After taking care of business in the bathroom, he climbed back into bed and pulled her into his arms. "This time we go slower. Deal?"

"Deal."

CHAPTER SEVEN

London stepped outside of a gym in the Brookhaven area, still feeling short of breath from her hour of cardio on the elliptical and half an hour of strength training. It also didn't help that the pollen in the air was higher than usual, which was something she hadn't missed while living in Charlotte. She'd had to use her inhaler more in the last two days than she had in the last few months while living out of state. Trying to keep her asthma in control was so far the only negative about the relocation. But the positives definitely outweighed the negatives.

A smile spread across her mouth as she jogged across the narrow road to the parking lot. A sizzle of warmth filled her just thinking about Mason. The last couple of months of dating had exceeded her expectations and she loved him more than she thought possible. She couldn't ever remember being as happy as she was at that moment.

Mason had said on more than one occasion that he wished they hadn't waited so long to hook up. But they definitely made up for lost time. He had adjusted his work schedule, which made the difference in them spending a few days together during the week to almost every day now. What London loved most was the companionship he provided—something that she'd been missing in her life. There were also great perks that came with dating him. Like his sweet kisses, his bear hugs, and no way could she forget his creativity in the bedroom.

Still grinning like a little kid who had just swiped cookies from the cookie jar, London opened the trunk and placed her gym bag inside. She had decided to work out in Brookhaven before going home, since she wanted to pick up a few items from Costco, which shared a parking lot.

Double checking to make sure she had her membership card, she slammed the trunk closed and maneuvered between parked cars to the next aisle. While strolling toward the store, she thought about how her life was finally coming together. She was back home around friends and family, doing the job she'd always dreamed of and dating her favorite guy.

"London?"

She slowed her steps as unease clawed down her back.

No. No. No. There was no way he could be there. There was no way the familiar voice she just heard, belonged to who she thought it might belong to. London debated on turning around, but then her name was called again.

Heart banging hard against her ribcage, she braced herself as she slowly turned.

Cory.

"I thought that was you." He approached her smiling, as if they were the best of friends. London gripped her keys tighter in her palm, her car key between her fingers in the ready, in case she needed a weapon.

"What are you doing here?" Fear now turned to anger. She never thought that she would one day hate this man, but hate wasn't a strong enough word to describe what she felt deep inside of her heart. He had made her life a living hell during the last six months she lived in North Carolina. If he thought she was going to wither into a crumbling mess, he had another thing coming. She wasn't running anymore. "What are you doing here?" she repeated, emphasizing each word.

"Actually, I'm in town on business. I'm staying in Buckhead and figured I'd come to this gym." Dressed in workout gear, the sleeveless T-shirt showed just how fit he was, his bare, muscular arms on full display.

"What about you? What are you doing in Atlanta?"

Slow to respond, London had a nagging feeling that he knew. It was too much of a coincidence that he happened to be in Atlanta and at the same gym. There was also something in his eyes that said he knew.

"Wait." He snapped his fingers, ignoring her questions. "I think I did hear that you had relocated. I'm a little disappointed that you didn't tell me you were leaving town. Despite how things ended between us, I'll always love you and want what's best for you. Hopefully you didn't move because of our breakup."

He stepped forward and she took two giant steps back until she bumped into the rear of a parked car. Unable to stop the trembling coursing through her body, she focused on her breathing … which seemed harder to do the longer she stood there.

Chuckling, Cory shook his head. "Still as skittish as a little mouse, huh? Well, I'd better get in here and get my workout in. Good seeing you again. Take care of yourself." He turned and walked away whistling.

London didn't know how long she stood there shaking, her heart pounding as if it were going to leap out of her body. She wasn't sure on whether to go into the store or head back to her car. Fear kept her immobile.

Why did she keep allowing him to get into her head? This was just some sick, twisted game to him. He wanted her to know, just because she had removed him from her life, didn't mean he couldn't show up whenever and wherever he wanted.

London jumped and whirled around when a car horn blew. *This is ridiculous.* She was not going to give him power over her. Instead of going back to the car, she rushed across the parking lot to the Costco building.

Okay, just calm down. She tried slowing her rapid heart rate. Looking around, she saw there was no sign of Cory, but she didn't trust him. Then again, if he really wanted to do anything to her, he had plenty of opportunities while in Charlotte. And also moments ago. Maybe she was overreacting.

"Excuse me."

London glanced up, not realizing she was standing in the way of two women trying to get shopping carts.

"Oh. I-I'm sorry." She moved out of the way, but stayed near the building, not ready to go inside. Her hands shook as she pulled out her cell phone, needing to talk to someone. Anyone.

Stilling her nerves, her fingers hovered over the screen. If she called Mason, like she'd thought about doing, he'd be there in a heartbeat, despite what he might have going on. If she called Harper, she would call Mason.

London's phone rang and she startled, her freehand resting on her chest as if that would slow her heart down.

Pull it together, girl.

When the phone rang two more times, she glanced at the screen. A wave of relief flooded her body when she saw Mason's name.

"Hello," she answered, sounding out of breath.

"Hey, baby, where are you?"

She swallowed and stared across the parking lot at L.A. Fitness. *Nothing happened*, she reminded herself. There was no need to tell Mason anything. He would only freak out and start hovering over her like he'd done for weeks after finding out about Cory.

"I'm at Costco. I wanted to pick up a few items before heading home."

Silence.

"Hello?" She tried to sound upbeat when Mason didn't say anything more.

"You okay? You don't sound like yourself and I still hear a little bit of wheezing."

London shook her head. Maybe his military training taught him to pick up on every small detail. In his defense, though, she had been waking up the last couple of nights coughing and wheezing. Of course he was ready to rush her to the hospital each time, fearing she was having an asthma attack. But normally after a couple of puffs from her inhaler, she settled down.

"I'm fine. The pollen seems to be a little higher today. I was thinking about cooking tonight. Do you want to come over to Harper's place later?"

London peeked around the parking lot again, not seeing Cory. Maybe he was telling the truth. Maybe he really was in town on business. It wasn't totally unrealistic since his tech job often had him traveling to Georgia, Alabama, and sometimes South Carolina quarterly on business.

"Aren't you tired? Why don't you come over here and I'll take care of dinner?"

"You can't cook. Or have you forgotten?" London cracked.

"I didn't say I would cook. I said I'd take care of dinner."

She chuckled, still vigilant in looking out for Cory.

"What's your ETA?"

Her brows drew together. "My what?"

"Your estimated time of arrival."

She laughed and changed her mind about picking up a few items from the store. He was right. She was tired. What she really wanted to do was take a bubble bath and then curl up next to him.

London hurried to her BMW while she was still talking to Mason. Even having him on the phone gave her a sense of security while she dodged between cars.

"Give me an hour." Climbing into the car, she quickly locked the doors. "I need to stop by Harp's place and grab some clothes."

"All right, baby, see you in a few. Love you." Mason disconnected.

London stared at her cell phone, her mouth hanging open. Had she heard him right? No way had he just said the "L" word.

She finally closed her mouth but still sat dumbfounded, trying to wrap her mind around the fact that he'd said he loved her. That was a first.

A slow smile spread across her lips and she held her phone close to her chest. She had loved Mason for as long as she could remember, but hadn't expected the declaration from him, at least not yet. But ...

"Okay, calm down. Don't get too excited," she coached herself after a few minutes and started the car.

Mason's words could have just slipped out. *They might not have been planned.* But then again, maybe he did mean them. "Well, we'll see. If he meant the words, it wouldn't be the last time he used them."

*

Ah damn, Mason thought as he shoved his cell phone into his pocket and blew out a ragged breath. He leaned against the wall in the back hallway of the club that led up to the offices. Had he really just said *love you*? Never had he ever slipped up like that with a woman. Not even in the heat of passion.

He turned to head up the stairs but stopped before he took the first step. Cursing under his breath, he dropped back against the wall when he saw his brother in the middle of the staircase, a stupid grin on his face.

"Did I just hear what I think I heard?" his brother asked, trotting down the stairs. Mason was surprised to see Cameron since he was rarely at the club these days. Spending so much time with Simone had lightened his mood and Mason couldn't ever remember seeing his brother smile as much as he did lately. "Did you just tell a certain someone that you loved her?"

Mason said nothing. What could he say? That he was crazy in love with a woman who he'd known forever but never thought he would have such strong feelings for?

"Did you mean it? Are you in love with her?"

"Yes," he answered simply. No sense in denying what he knew in his heart was true. He was in love with London Alexander. The reality didn't freak him out as much as it probably should have. He wanted them to get better acquainted mainly to see if they got along well enough to have children together. Now, he wanted more. But how much more was the question.

"By the panicked look on your face, I take it that was the first time you've spoken the words to her."

Heck, it was the first time Mason had spoken those words to any woman who wasn't in his immediate family.

Cameron made it to the bottom step. "You do know that you're going to have to tell her for real so that she doesn't think the words were a slip up, don't you?"

Mason's brow's drew together. "What do you mean? Why would she think it was a slip?"

"Because you haven't told her how you feel. Yet, all of sudden, you throw out 'love you' in a telephone call and then hang up."

Mason was way out of his element on the subject. He had never been in love with a woman before.

"If you love her, tell her. Let her know how you feel so that she doesn't start acting weird, wondering if you really meant the words, but are afraid to bring up the subject." Cameron pounded him on the shoulder and headed out of the building. "Good luck. I'm outta here."

Mason continued up the stairs. His brother was probably right, but now Mason would be forced to talk about love.

Relationships. This was why he stayed clear of anything serious.

CHAPTER EIGHT

London watched from the bleachers inside the Boys & Girls Club as Mason ran up and down the basketball court with middle schoolers. He volunteered once a week and today he planned a summer pizza party for the kids. London's heart swelled with how much she admired him for giving some of his time to children. Many of them were growing up without a positive male role model in their life and he felt he could make a difference.

London glanced at her watch and shifted on the bench. She had arrived a few minutes ago. While Mason's visit was all about the children, she was there in a work capacity to do a piece about the club's summer programming.

London looked up in time to see Mason dunk the basketball, hanging on the rim longer than necessary. She smiled as the kids went wild, cheering him on. He was in his element around them and they adored him. The girls hung onto his every word, while the boys tried to be cool like him, imitating his movements and expressions.

When the game ended, Mason grabbed a towel and wiped his face. Then he headed her way.

"I see you're still a showboat on the basketball court."

"Hey, what can I say? When you're good, you're good."

Laughing, London rolled her eyes. The first two years of high school, he had played on the varsity basketball team. During that second year, he hurt his knee and was sidelined for the season, but that didn't stop the girls from fawning over him. Mason ate up the attention.

"Come with me." Mason reached for her hand and guided her down the three rickety bleacher stairs.

"Where are we going?"

"You'll see."

"I don't want to go too far because my cameraman will be here soon. I don't want him to wonder if I'm here."

"You worry too much. Come on." They stepped out of the gym and into the main hallway where groups of children and volunteers were congregated. Saying hello as they went by, Mason ushered her down another hall which was empty.

"Mase, where are we going?" she asked again, her curiosity piqued.

He glanced over his shoulder without responding and then opened a door. "In here."

Frowning, she stepped into the cramped space. "A broom closet? Really?"

He grinned and then pulled her close. "I didn't get a chance to properly greet you when you strolled in."

He lowered his head and his lips touched hers, sending heat rushing through her body down to the soles of her feet. Each time he kissed her, she fell deeper in love. A whimper rattled in her throat when he ended the kiss.

"Besides, it's too noisy out there. I wanted someplace private for us to talk." His tone was more serious than moments ago.

Brooms, dustpans, and mops hung neatly on the wall, and several empty buckets were on the floor of the small space. London didn't see any cleaning products, but a hint of pine lingered in the air.

When Mason continued to study her without speaking, she asked, "Do the kids know about the pizza party that you have planned?" Her hands glided up his chest, his T-shirt damp against her palms. What she really wanted to ask was if he meant the words he had spoken to her the day before.

"Most of them know. I've been planning this for a while." He ran the back of his hand down the side of her cheek, staring into her eyes. "What time is the news crew going to arrive?"

"Around three. Are you sure you're okay with me infringing on your time here with the kids? I just thought that since I was going to meet you here anyway, that this might be a good opportunity to shed light on the club."

"I'm fine with it."

"I know I could have picked another day, but this was perfect timing since I've been working on the summer break series. This will give me a chance to highlight some of the programs and hopefully create more community involvement for them. Besides that, some parents might not have even thought about sending their bored children here for the summer. But I don't have to capture the party or—"

"Hey," Mason kissed her lips, "you don't have to convince me. I think it's a great idea. And no, I don't feel as if you're infringing on my time with the kids."

There she went rambling again. London didn't know why she was suddenly nervous. This would be the third segment of the Summertime in Atlanta series and the first two installments had great viewership. Even though they were deep into summer, the information could still be helpful to parents. Especially since the Boys & Girls Club offered activities for kids year-round. She'd been surprised when her boss asked her to host the short series. Once she had accepted the anchor position, she didn't think she'd get an opportunity to go out on location again.

She took a few cleansing breaths and glanced away from Mason's piercing gaze. Her anxiousness wasn't just about the segment. She had tossed and turned all night, still unable to get over seeing Cory again. The sight of him had scared her, but he hadn't seemed threatening like the other times.

"What's on your mind?" Mason touched her chin with the tip of his finger, forcing her to look at him. "London?" he said when she didn't speak.

"Why do you ask?" What the heck? Was he reading minds now?

"Because you were quiet when you got to my place last night and you barely slept. This morning you seemed a little … I don't know, distracted maybe."

Was he trying to get her to start the conversation about his profession of love? Or what if he hadn't even realized he said the words? Or did he sense that something had happened? Was she giving off some type of fear vibe?

"I'm okay."

"I didn't ask if you were okay. I asked if something happened yesterday."

"Nah, not really. It was just a long day. I'm still trying to get acclimated at work. I'm hoping the segment will help to not only shed awareness on the Boys & Girls Club, as well as help me get some notoriety with the station. Their ratings have been staggering lately and they are trying different techniques to get them up."

When Mason didn't respond, London glanced at him. She could feel the tension seeping from his pores. No way was she telling him that she saw Cory. The guy barely gave her a second thought anyway. Maybe he really was in town on business.

"Would you tell me if something was going on?" Mason asked as if reading her mind again.

"With us? Of course. As far as I'm concerned, we're fine." Except that he'd tossed out 'love you' and she didn't know if there was meaning behind the words or if it were a slip of the tongue.

London shook her head. Why was she tripping? Their relationship was new, and there were days that she still couldn't believe that she and Mason Bennett were dating. Well, sort of. He was willing for them to get to know each other for the sole purpose of deciding whether or not to make a baby together, but still. She really believed that in time, he would fall madly in love with her and want her for more than just his baby's momma. Maybe she was being naïve, but what she wanted more than anything was to have a family of her own.

"I'm not talking about just us, Tiny. If something is going on with you, I want you to tell me." He cupped her cheek. "No matter what it is. Okay?"

She hesitated and leaned into his touch, a warmth spreading through her like sunshine after a rainy day. "Okay."

*

Mason was convinced London was hiding something. Was she having second thoughts about them? Or had Cameron been right? His brother had never steered him wrong, though they rarely talked about matters of the heart.

After kissing London again, Mason reached for the doorknob, but stopped. "About what I said yesterday," he started, unsure of the unchartered direction in which the conversation was going. Staring into her eyes gave him the encouragement he needed to proceed. "I love you. Granted the words came out yesterday without me really thinking about them, but I meant them."

Her smile was wide and her eyes teary, but she didn't cry. Thank God. If there was one thing he realized he couldn't handle, it was seeing her cry. He didn't care if they were happy tears. He didn't want to see them.

"I love you, too." She moved closer and looped her arms around his waist. "I've loved you for as long as I can remember and hearing you tell me that ..."

Instead of finishing, she stood on tiptoe and Mason met her the rest of the way. He would never get tired of kissing her sweet lips. Devouring their softness, he cupped her face between his hands, taking all that she was giving. Every day she captured more and more of his heart.

Lifting his mouth from hers, he gazed into her eyes. "Are you really okay?"

"I'm fine. Really. We're fine."

He said nothing. Their relationship started a little unconventional, but she meant more to him than he could ever express. But right now he hoped the 'I'm fine' meant exactly that and not code for 'you better sleep with one eye open if you wait too much longer to put a ring on it'. He had every intention of moving forward in getting to know all there was to know about her. They were great together and right now, he couldn't imagine himself with anyone else.

London turned to leave. "Okay, let's get out of here before I jump your bones."

Laughing, Mason caught her by the waist and lifted her off the floor. Despite her surprise, her legs went around him automatically and he backed her up against the wall.

"You cannot say stuff like that and think I can let you out of here without doing a little somethin' somethin'."

London giggled and wiggled against him while he nuzzled her neck and squeezed her butt, which fit perfectly in his palms. "We can't. Not here. Not with all of those kids out there and probably my cameraman. Now stop. Let me down. We can pick this up later."

"In a broom closet?"

London laughed again and shook her head. "If you can find one where there are no kids around, then maybe. Now put me down. I have work to do."

She groaned as Mason slid her slowly down his body, wanting her to feel the effect she had on him. He was like a horny teenager whenever he was within an inch of her, his body responding immediately. Yeah, they were definitely going to pick this up later. Now all he had to do was find a secluded broom closet.

CHAPTER NINE

The next day, London drove around the block one more time before she finally noticed a parking spot on the street, several doors down from the café. She was meeting Harper for an early lunch not too far from the television station.

London pulled up to the side of a car to parallel park, hoping she could fit her BMW into the tight space. After two attempts, she finally parked and hurried out of the vehicle.

"Here, let me get that for you," an older gentleman with a short afro and graying near his temples said, opening the door to the café. "I love holding the door for lovely women."

London graced him with a smile. "Thank you." As she walked into the eclectic café, her gaze immediately took in the dark walls, laden with abstract art. The burnt red, polished, concrete floors could barely be seen since there were small tables and chairs covering almost every square inch.

London spotted Harper in a far corner and headed her way.

"Hey, girl." Harper stood and hugged her. "Did you find the place okay?"

"I did. Although for a minute there, I didn't think I would find a parking spot."

"Yeah, I should have warned you about the parking around here. I thought with us meeting early, there wouldn't be a problem, but I had to park almost a block away."

For the next few minutes, while glancing at the menu, they chatted about the neighborhood—a revitalization area—as well as their morning.

"Today must be my lucky day," the server stated when he stepped next to their table. The Don Cheadle look alike, with a diamond stud in his left ear and a huge toothy smile, pulled out his note pad. "I get not one, but two gorgeous women at my table. Clearly I have died and gone to heaven."

"Don't start with the flirting, Todd. We're both spoken for," Harper said before taking a sip from her water glass.

He grabbed his chest. "Harper, you wound me. Why do you insist on ruining my day?" He teased with them for a while before taking their order and then headed to the next table.

"Considering we live in the same house, I rarely see you," Harper said after Todd walked away.

"That's because you spend all of your free time with the Hunt man," London cracked. Harper and Hunter were still going strong and London couldn't be happier for her friend.

"Me? What about you? I can't get any time with my girl because my brother is hogging up all of your free time."

"I know." London grinned, unable to help herself. She definitely missed her girl time with Harper. Yet, the last few months with Mason had been some of the best months of her life.

"I have to admit, at first I was afraid that Mase was sticking close to you because of Cory, but that's definitely not the case anymore. Seems like he's found a much better reason."

London shrugged off the comment, feeling guilty for not telling Harper about running into Cory near the gym the other day. If she told Harper, then Harper would tell Mason and they both knew him well enough to know he'd overreact. Technically, Cory hadn't done anything to her except make her uncomfortable. London hadn't seen or heard anything else from him, but Mason wouldn't look at it like that. He would not only insist on driving her everywhere, he would go after Cory. Which wouldn't help anyone.

He was a trained killer with a short fuse when it came to anyone bothering his family or his woman.

The last thought made her smile. Deep down she loved his protective nature. With him, she not only felt safe, but she felt loved.

"I guess that huge smile lighting up your face means that you and Mase are getting along well," Harper said just before Todd came back with their meals.

"Okay, ladies. I have the strawberry spinach salad for you," he placed a large bowl of mixed greens and fruit in front of Harper, "and for you, my new favorite customer, I—"

"Wait. I thought I was your favorite." Harper feigned offense. "You don't even know her and already she's your favorite?"

"Look at her," Todd pointed at London with his free hand, "she's absolutely stunning. Not saying that you're not, but now that you're taken ..."

"She's taken, too, and her man is the jealous type."

"Duly noted." Todd set London's plate in front of her and winked before leaving the table.

"So do you two carry on like that all the time?" London cut into her pecan crusted chicken.

"Girl, yes. He's a sweetheart and harmless. But let's get back to you."

"Mase used the 'L' word the other day."

"Whaaat?" Harper's mouth remained opened, but she quickly recovered and squealed. "I knew it! But, I don't know why I'm acting so surprised. He's always had feelings for you even if he didn't know it. So tell me everything."

They ate and talked as London gave Harper a play-by-play of her conversation with Mason. Though it felt a little weird talking to Harper about her brother, London kept going. She didn't have anyone else to share with and no one knew her and Mason better than Harper.

"I'm glad that knuckle-headed brother of mine finally admitted his feelings for you. Now to get him to propose marriage so we can go wedding-dress shopping."

London set her fork down. "Harp, don't start."

Harper pointed her fork at London. "I don't care what you say. Mason loves you, spends all of his time with you, and will kill anyone who steps to you. He had better marry you."

"Well, don't pick out your maid of honor dress yet. He's still not interested in having a wife."

"Then you're going to have to practice tough love and walk away. I still think you were crazy to offer to have children with him without marriage in the first place. The only reason I backed off was because Mason has always had strong feelings for you. Normally I don't believe a woman can change a man, but if anyone can change Mason's opinion about commitment and marriage, it's you."

London wanted nothing more than to be Mrs. Mason Bennett, but she wouldn't hold her breath. Mason made it clear that he still wasn't looking to get married and she planned to respect his decision.

She moved food around on her plate with her fork, no longer hungry. Normally she would agree with Harper about walking away since Mason didn't want what she wanted. If she had a list of stupidest things she'd ever done over the years, propositioning Mason would rank number one. Going along with *his* proposition was the second stupidest. She should've known she couldn't handle dating him without any expectations. But it was too late. She was in too deep.

*

Mason leaned on the console in Club Masquerade's control room, studying some of the monitors. Spending much of his time lately with London, he hadn't been at the club as often. Fortunately, he could rely on their great staff. From what he could see everything seemed to be running smoothly.

"When we get the new equipment, maybe we can consider adding an extra camera near the side bar," Jack, one of the security specialists, said. He and three other people were monitoring the comings and goings of the club. "What we have now is okay, but I think one more behind where Ted is standing will give us more eyes on the area to his left."

Mason followed Jack's hand as he pointed to various spots on the overhead monitors. "I agree. We'll have a few extra cameras when it's all said and done, and we can identify any other areas that might need more of our attention."

"Mase?" Hamilton's voice boomed through a covert earpiece Mason wore while on site.

"Yeah. Go ahead, Ham."

"Don't trip, but there's a guy at the round bar who's been watching your girl's table since they arrived. I'm thinking London is the object of his affection because when she was on the dance floor, he stood off to the side watching her until she returned to the table."

Tension crawled down Mason's back and he moved down the console to the monitor that he could best see London. She and some of her coworkers had arrived about an hour ago, taking advantage of Wind Down Wednesday happy hour. He was surprised to see her since she'd been pulling some long hours at work for the last couple of days.

Mason's gaze scanned the bar. The lighting on the first floor of the club wasn't as dark during happy hour as they had it sometimes on the weekend, but he still had to look closely. "Which guy?"

"The one in a striped shirt, sleeves rolled up to his elbow, nursing a beer. His back is to the circular stairs."

Mason stood over his security guy's shoulder, staring at the man Hamilton described. "Zoom in on him," he said to the guy monitoring that screen.

"Dammit," Mason growled.

Cory.

The dossier Wiz had sent over about Cory Fields included a more recent photo than the one London had showed him two years earlier.

Mason had no idea what the guy was up to, but he had every intention of finding out. His attention went back to where London sat. She was finally starting to seem like her old self. She enjoyed her job, and no longer had the stress of looking for a place to live since Harper suggested that they live together for a while longer. The last thing he wanted was for London to know that Cory was in town. He also didn't want to risk her seeing him if he went down and snatched the guy up.

"Ham, see if you can lure him to the back stairs without raising attention. I don't want London to see him."

Mason watched as Hamilton approached the guy and whispered into his ear, Bones hanging out nearby. Words were exchanged back and forth. This was one of those times when he appreciated Hamilton's patience. He knew himself well enough to know he wouldn't bother with a lot of words. He wasn't patient with assholes who harassed defenseless women.

Cory turned his beer bottle up. Looking to finish it off, he set it on the bar and finally stood. Hamilton led him the long way around the club to the 'Personnel Only' area, away from London, with Bone's pulling up the rear.

Mason buttoned his suit jacket, concealing his holster, and headed toward the stairs. He had no idea what he was going to say to the guy, but he had to convince him that, one: he wasn't welcomed at the club. And two: if Mason found him anywhere near London again, he would be sorry.

"What do you mean there's been a complaint?" Cory growled the moment they were in the private hallway and

Mason was midway down the stairs. "What type of complaint?"

Mason had wondered what Hamilton had said to Cory to get him to follow him out.

"The table of women in the corner that you've been watching felt uncomfortable with you staring at them," Hamilton explained without looking at Mason.

Cory gave a humorless laugh. "This is crazy. So what, I can't admire beautiful women?"

"Not when one of those women belong to me," Mason said, from the stairwell. "Cory Fields, right?" Mason stood in front of the guy wanting like hell to punch him. At around six feet tall with a muscular build, Cory looked as if he could hold his own. But Mason had full-blown anger on his side. The thought that a man this size had manhandled London, made him want to squeeze the life out of him.

Cory narrowed his eyes. "Who are you?"

"Doesn't matter."

"It matters when you step to me like this!" Cory took a half a step back when Mason got in his face. "I don't know what this is about, but you need to check yourself, brotha."

"I'm not your brotha. And as for London ..." Mason noticed a flicker in Cory's eyes at the mention of her name, but it disappeared as quick as it appeared. "She is off limits to you. I don't know what type of sick game you're playing, but I suggest you head back to North Carolina and forget about her."

A slow smirk lifted the corner of Cory's lips. "And if I don't?"

Anger boiled inside of Mason. He snatched the guy up by the front of his shirt and slammed him against the wall. With his forearm against the man's neck, cutting off his airway, Mason knew that if he didn't let up some, he'd kill him on the spot. Before loosening his grip, their noses almost touching, Mason said, "If you don't, I will hunt you down and beat your motherfucking ass."

"I ca-can't brea—" Cory gasped for air, his hands grasping at Mason's arm.

Hamilton gripped Mason's shoulder. "Mase. Let him go."

"Not until I'm sure he understands how serious I am." His voice was low and threatening. Cory's eyes closed, his breaths shallow. Mason didn't care. He placed his mouth near the man's ear. "If you call her, if you come anywhere near her, if you put your hands on her again … I'm coming for you."

"Mason, let him go," Hamilton repeated.

Mason jerked his arm to the side, throwing the guy to the travertine floor. He stood over Cory, watching him cough and gasp for air.

"Come near her again and your ass is mine."

CHAPTER TEN

"You're still not sounding too good. Are you sure you can handle another couple of hours at work?" Mason asked.

London closed a folder that she'd been looking through, shoving it back into the file drawer to her right. Mason had been hovering over her, staying closer than a shadow since her asthma had flared up the day before. But London had a feeling his overprotectiveness had nothing to do with her health.

"I'm fine, Mase. But are *you* all right? You've been acting a little strange. Well, stranger than usual."

"Ha, ha, ha, very funny. I'm cool. But I'm not the one who is still wheezing. Although you do sound better than you did yesterday, but not much. I'm actually surprised your boss didn't send you home."

"My producer suggested I take the rest of the day off, but I told him I'd be fine."

London hadn't been there long enough to start taking days off. Battling asthma wasn't new to her. She had dealt with the illness all her life and knew the warning signs of an attack. The flare-ups concerned her, but as long as she had her rescue inhaler nearby, she wasn't worried.

"Well, don't forget to call me before you leave work."

"Mase, what's going on?" Now she knew something was up. He had insisted on driving her to work the last few days and she gave in. Today, she drove herself since she had to be at work by three that morning and he hadn't gotten home until one. Since her first break, he'd either called or texted her to check in.

"Nothing's going on. I know you haven't been feeling well and I want to make sure you're all right."

London hesitated. "Okay, if you're sure."

"So you're going to call me?"

"Yes, I'll call you."

"Good. I'll talk to you later. Love you."

"Love you more." She smiled and disconnected. She wouldn't ever get tired of hearing those words from him. Not only did he say them often, but on a daily basis he showed her how important she was to him.

Dating Mason had taken some getting used to since he had always treated her like a little sister. There were days she still had to pinch herself to know that this was real life. She had dreamt about being his woman for as long as she could remember. But now, being with him felt as normal as opening her eyes every morning.

Yep, they were going to make it. They were great together.

Hours later, London rushed from the ladies' room ignoring the tightness in her chest and headed for the anchor desk. She was supposed to be in her seat ten minutes before go time and she was late.

She dropped down in her seat and blew out an exhausted breath, coughing again. She dabbed at the perspiration near her hairline. This was her last on-air hour for the day, and she prayed she could get through it without breathing hard and coughing.

"You feeling okay?" her co-anchor whispered when London coughed once more, a wheeze following close behind.

She shook her head but said, "Yeah, I think so." Breathing in slowly, she tried holding back another cough, annoyed at herself that she didn't stop by her cubicle for her inhaler, but ...

London glanced up at the countdown clock on top of the camera. She patted her hair, hoping it was still in place, and attached her mic with only three minutes left before going live. *Relax*. She took the last couple of minutes to focus on her breathing.

Four. Three. Two. One.

"Good afternoon every ... one, I'm London Ale ... xander," she wheezed, anxiousness coursing through her veins as she read the teleprompter. "New at five, po ... lice broke up a drug ring in Buck ... head this after ... noon. Let's ... go to Jesse Ch-Chase who is stan ... ding by live near Peachtree Road."

London struggled to breathe in and out without coughing. Her producer spoke into her ear, letting her know she should leave the set. The tightness in London's chest and the struggle to breathe grew as she pushed back in her seat.

An intern rushed over. "What's wrong?" He assisted her with removing the microphone and earpiece before helping her away from the desk.

"In ... haler. I need ... my ... inhaler." She coughed and wheezed with every word.

"Where is it?" His gaze darted around when they arrived in London's cubicle.

She yanked open the desk draw and grabbed her rescue inhaler and collapsed into her chair. Shaking the device a few times she brought it to her mouth.

"Better?" the intern, who was now bent down in front of her, asked a few seconds after she took a second puff.

"Yes. Thank you." She coughed.

London glanced up to find several of her co-workers and producer standing in the opening of the cubicle.

"I'm sorry," she hurried to say. Deep down she knew she shouldn't have gone on air, but she honestly thought she could handle the last hour.

"All that matters is that you're okay," the producer said after London's co-workers expressed their concern before going back to work. "I should have insisted you take the rest of the day off earlier."

London shook her head, still feeling a little winded. "No. It's my fault. This flare-up kinda caught me off guard."

The intern returned holding a cup. "My mother has asthma and hot tea seems to help her no matter how hot it is outside."

London flashed him a smile. "Thank you. This is very thoughtful." Hot tea had helped her in the past, too, but she hadn't thought to make a cup today.

"Take it easy for a while and then I want you to head home." The producer turned to the intern. "Hang out with her until she's feeling better. Then call a car for her."

"That's not necessary. I'll be all right and I drove." When he started to speak again, she added, "I won't leave until I know I'm feeling well enough to drive. But thank you both for everything."

The producer hesitated. "Okay, but if you're not feeling better before you're ready to leave, let us know and we'll get you home. And take tomorrow off as well."

London agreed. Sipping the hot tea, which tasted as if it had a hint of honey, she debated on whether to go home or stick around until she felt better. Deciding on the latter, she finished her tea, and rested her head against the back of the chair before closing her eyes. Focusing on her breathing, she tried relaxing. She needed to figure out why her asthma kept acting up. Blaming it on the pollen count wouldn't fly anymore since the last few days the pollen had been fine. Maybe it was time to change her medication. She wasn't sure, but no way was she going to risk an asthma attack on television again.

After a short nap, London glanced at her cell phone, surprised she'd slept for forty-five minutes. She changed out of her heels and slipped into the flats that she'd worn earlier. Getting off of work a little early would give her time to cook dinner before Mason stopped by. Then again, since she was still a little tired, maybe she would have him order in.

Thinking about him reminded her that she needed to call him. She pulled out her cell phone, but instead of calling, she sent him a quick text.

I'm heading home. See you later.

London didn't wait for a response and left her cubicle.

"Hope you feel better."

"See you next week."

Her co-workers said as she passed them, heading to the exit that would take her to the parking lot.

"Thank you. Have a good evening."

It had been a long time since she had to leave work due to not feeling well. So the next few days would be used to rest up. Hopefully she could get a doctor's appointment soon. Her medication hadn't changed in years, but maybe it was time.

London said her good-byes to a few more people

before slipping on her sunglasses. Pushing the door to the parking lot open, she braced herself for the heat. The temperature had been in the mid-nineties for the past week and today was no different. The humidity felt as if it was at a thousand percent, perspiration popped out along her hairline.

She dug through the side pocket of her large handbag and pulled out her keys.

"London."

London turned back. A smile played on her lips when the fashionista of the television station waved. Tabitha, one of the floor directors, was the first person to befriend London when she started. Strolling back toward her, London admired the short, sleeveless peplum dress and stylish high heels. Tabitha had mentioned having a dinner date that evening and whoever she was meeting was in for a treat because she looked amazing.

Tabitha hugged her. "Hey, I heard you had an asthma attack. Are you okay?"

"It wasn't an actual attack. Lately, my asthma has been acting up, but I feel better. Thanks for asking."

"Oh no problem. I love that bag." She pointed to London's light blue Coach handbag, a birthday present to herself the year before.

"Thank you. I'm trying to keep up with you." She nodded to Tabitha's huge Michael Kors duffle bag in one hand and purse in the other.

"Oh, girl, please. Me and the outlet stores are very good friends." They both laughed and talked for a few minutes longer before saying their good-byes.

Turning down the aisle where her car was parked, London's steps slowed.

What the …

Two flat tires.

So much for getting home early. Now she had to wait for a tow truck.

Still staring at the car, London realized the vehicle wasn't leaning to one side as it should, considering the flat tires. She took a look on the other side of the car and froze. All four tires flat.

"Ugh, today of all ..." Wait. No way could she have four flat tires. With a closer look at one of the wheels, she noticed the long slash in the face of the tire.

No. No. No.

Fear crawled down her back and she backed away from the vehicle, glancing around frantically, gripping her purse strap tighter. *This can't be happening.* Her heart pounded like a jackhammer. She walked quickly toward the building, but started running when she got closer, glancing over her shoulder.

London didn't know how or when, but she had a sinking feeling that she knew who.

*

Mason sat listening as Malik Lewis, co-owner of Supreme Security Agency out of Chicago, explained his idea of how he, Mason, and Wiz could move forward with a partnership. Supreme provided personal security, as well as building security. The plan was to expand the agency to Atlanta, in which Mason would oversee the business and become part owner.

At about 6'8" and a retired Navy SEAL, Malik was a force to be reckoned with whether in the jungles of Iran or in the business world. He and Malik had met a few years back when they sat on a covert military joint task force. The group was comprised of retired and active duty military personnel. Becoming friends, they discussed one day going into business together. Malik started the

119

security agency, but Mason had reenlisted, putting his security business plan on hold.

Mason toyed with the empty water bottle in his hand. The dream of owning a security firm was coming to fruition. Granted, he would have partners, but he couldn't think of a better group of men to work with.

Malik leaned on the back of a guest chair in Cameron's office. "So what do you think?" They had started out in the club's security office where Malik had wanted to check on the installation his guys had done on the new security equipment.

Mason stood and stretched out his hand for a handshake. "Where do I sign?" He felt good about this decision. He would still oversee the security at Club Masquerade, while he continued to build upon the agency Malik and Wiz had already started.

"All right then. I'll finish drawing up the paperwork. I liked your idea of pulling from Atlanta's police department. We have former police officers on staff, but the majority of our security specialists have military backgrounds. I'll be sending Travis and Stan to Atlanta at the end of the year. They'll get your guys acclimated."

"That sounds good. I know it's going to take some time to get everything in order, and I welcome all the help I can get."

They headed down the stairs.

"You and your family have a real nice set up here. We might have to look into creating a night club similar to this in Chi-Town."

"Man, please. You have a one-year-old and another on the way. I doubt Natasha is going to go for you being pulled in yet another direction while she raises your kids."

Malik chuckled. "Good point. I already had to agree to no overnight trips unless she and my daughter come along. So having another one will definitely limit some of my travels. Even more reason why I'm glad you're onboard."

Listening to the loving way Malik talked about his family had Mason thinking about London. Malik, who was just as overprotective of his family as Mason was of his, had been happily married for three years. Though Mason couldn't see himself in the husband role, he respected any man who could make that type of commitment. Mason had met Natasha. As chief of staff of one of the largest hospitals in Chicago, she didn't take mess from no one, especially Malik.

"Well, man, I'd better get going if I want to make my flight," Malik said as they headed to the door that led to the employee parking lot. "But what about you? What's going on with London? Wiz mentioned how riled up you've been lately. She must be pretty special."

"Very special."

"Does that mean that you're ready to join the happily-married-husband club?"

Mason laughed, not answering the question. "I still can't believe you're married, and married to someone who could get you to stop cursing. Having a conversation with you that doesn't include a swear word every other sentence is nothing short of a miracle."

Back in the day, Malik was not only well known for his fight first and ask questions later mentality, but no one could string curse words together the way he could.

"What can I say? I married an angel. Not to say a curse word doesn't slip out on occasion. When our daughter dropped the 'F' bomb last week while playing with her toys, Tasha went off on me. I thought for sure she was going to leave my ass. Heck, she was so pissed, I may never use the 'F' word again."

Malik told a few more stories, clearly enthralled with his wife despite some of their misunderstandings. He and Wiz made marriage look easy, but Mason knew it wasn't. He had always tried to keep drama out of his personal life by never getting too serious with a woman. But now that London was in his life, he was starting to rethink a lot of things that he was once against.

Mason glanced at his watch, noting that London would be getting off of work soon. He still had time to call and make reservations at one of their favorite restaurants to surprise her with a romantic dinner.

He and Malik said their good-byes, promising to touch bases in a few weeks about next steps. *This is really going to happen.* All of his goals and desires were manifesting and Mason felt as if his life was really coming together.

He trotted back up the stairs and grabbed his suit jacket just as his cell phone vibrated. Glancing at the screen he smiled when he saw London's name.

"Hey, there. I was thinking about you. Wait. Shouldn't you be on the air?"

"Mase."

Mason stopped in the doorway of the security room. Worry rioted within him putting him on full alert at that one word. The shakiness in her voice had him holding his cell phone tighter.

"What's wrong?"

"Someone ... someone slashed my tires. All of them," she sobbed, and Mason's heart clenched. "I think he's here."

Mason knew immediately who she was referring to and flew back down the stairs. It was time to put a stop to this nonsense with Cory. "Where are you?"

"I'm still at work. I came outside to leave, but—"

"You're still outside?" he yelled. "Baby, please tell me you're inside of the building."

"I am. I didn't know what to do. One of my co-workers called the police and they're on their way."

"Good. Stay right there. I'm on my way."

CHAPTER ELEVEN

Two hours later, Mason pulled London into his arms and kissed the top of her head. He never again wanted to feel the gut-twisting ache that stabbed his heart when she first called. The fear in her voice shook him to his core. Worrying about his siblings and parents was one thing, but his concern for her... Mason couldn't even finish the thought. If anything ever happened to her, he would lose his shit.

He shook his head, willing the thought out of his mind. It had already taken him forever to admit his feelings, and he had no intentions of losing her.

After watching the security tapes at the television station, they were ninety-nine percent sure the person near her car, wearing a baseball cap pulled low over his eyes, was Cory. Now all they had to do was find him.

"You need to eat." Mason nudged London, prepared to force feed her if necessary. The little she'd told him that she had eaten for lunch wouldn't be enough to feed a fly. He was glad she wasn't still coughing, but he still heard a little wheeze rattle through her lungs whenever she spoke.

"I'm not hungry." She shifted against him on the sofa, placing her feet on the floor. After they left the station, she agreed to return to his loft with him. "I can't believe Cory did this to me. I just don't understand. He's never done anything like this before. Why trash my car now?"

Guilt stabbed Mason in the chest. He had no doubt that threatening Cory had prompted him to act out. Telling London about his encounter with her ex wasn't going to be easy.

"Even when I saw him, he didn't do anything. He only—"

"Whoa. Hold up. You saw him? Recently?" Unease crept through Mason. "When and where did you see him?"

Sighing, London leaned forward, her hands over her face and her elbows on her thighs. "I was leaving the gym in Brookhaven, the day before the pizza party. Cory was in the parking lot, saying that he was in town on business."

"Dammit, London! And you didn't think you should tell me? The guy has been basically stalking you and—"

"And I haven't seen him in months, Mason. Even when I saw him then, he didn't do anything. He was as surprised to see me as I was to see him." She dropped back on the sofa and folded her arms across her chest.

"And you believe that?" When she didn't respond, all Mason could do was stare at her. He checked his temper, trying to understand. "After what this guy put you through, you honestly believe that he was in town on business? That he happened to be at the same gym at the same time as you? And this is all a coincidence?"

When she still didn't reply, Mason stood, tension now turning to full-blown fury. When he arrived at the television station, she couldn't stop shivering. Mason had feared she was going into shock. She was so shaken and withdrawn. Right now he didn't want to say or do anything that would upset her more. But a war raged within him that she hadn't thought it important to tell him about the encounter.

He moved to the floor to ceiling windows, his mind taking him back to that day. He remembered her sounding weird on the telephone, but thought it had something to do with her asthma. That had been the same day he blurted out 'love you'.

He ran his hand over his mouth and down his chin. He couldn't be mad at her for not saying anything since he hadn't told her about his confrontation with Cory.

Mason turned from the window. Instead of reclaiming his seat, he sat on the coffee table in front of the sofa, facing her.

"It's my fault," she started. "I should have talked to him, asked why he's been harassing me. I should have—"

"I saw Cory at Club Masquerade a few days ago. He was sitting at the bar staring at you and some of your co-workers." Mason considered not telling her the rest, but he had to. "And I might have threatened to hurt him if he came anywhere near you."

London slowly unfolded her arms and leaned forward, their faces only inches apart. Mason swallowed. If looks could kill, he would have shriveled into a mound of ashes right then and there. He had only seen her angry a few times, but not like this. Not when he could feel the fury bouncing off of her.

"Might have? You might have threatened him? You saw him and you didn't think it important to tell *me*?"

Realization showed in her eyes. "Is that why you've been acting so weird? Did you know he was going to come after me?"

Mason narrowed his eyes. "What do you mean come after you? Are we talking about more than the tires here? Did you see him today?" He gripped the edge of the table. "Please don't lie to me, London."

Her mouth dropped open. "I would never lie to you, Mase. Never!"

He almost said omission was the same as lying, but kept his mouth shut. He hadn't been any better.

"And no, I haven't seen Cory since that day in the gym's parking lot." She wrapped her arms around her midsection. "What if ... what if he would have done something to me while I was in the car? You should have warned me that you and he had words. I know it was naïve, but I wanted to believe he was only in town on business."

"I know." Mason rubbed his hands down her bare arms.

"I'm scared, Mason. If Cory could slash all of my tires, who knows what he could do to me." Her voice waivered.

"Aw, baby." Mason joined her on the sofa and pulled her close. He had wondered when she was going to finally break down. She'd been barely responsive at the television station, only responding with one word answers. He had expected to find her in tears when he arrived, but instead she was jumpy and quiet.

Mason pulled her onto his lap. "I will break every bone in Cory's body if he ever puts his hands on you. I will never let him hurt you. Never."

"But what are we going to do now?"

"We're going to find him."

"Let's let the police handle him. I would never forgive myself if something happened to you or you ended up in trouble trying to help me with this Cory situation."

Mason cupped her face. "Listen. Nothing's going to happen to me. But I have no respect or tolerance for men who bully women. Cory is twice your size. I can't even wrap my brain around how he can live with himself knowing that he's terrorizing you."

"I know you, Mase. Promise me you'll let the cops handle this. Cory's not worth it."

"He's screwing with your head. As long as he's out there, showing up unexpectedly, you'll never have peace. And you're too important to me for me to let this continue." Mason kissed the tip of her nose and ran his fingers through her short hair.

"He hasn't hurt me."

"And I want to keep it that way. When someone hurts you, they hurt me, and he'll pay with his life if he ever hurts you."

"Hearing you say stuff like that scares me more than Cory ever could."

Okay, he wouldn't say it again, but Mase meant every word. Cory was a dead man if he ever put his hands on her.

*

London woke the next morning, cocooned within Mason's strong arms, his steady snore interrupting the otherwise quiet room. Face-to-face with his smooth, muscular chest, she wanted to reach out and touch him, but refrained. Just because she was awake, didn't mean that he had to be.

She readjusted her head on his arm, but wasn't able to move the rest of her upper body thanks to his tight hold. She wasn't going to complain. Last night she appreciated him and his strength more than she cared to admit. For years she had taken care of herself, but having someone to lean on for a change was nice. Real nice.

She glanced up, using the moment to admire Mason's strong features. Her gaze flowed over his smooth, dark skin stretched over his broad nose and the ridge of his cheekbones. She went lower to his full, yummy lips. Lips that had explored her entire body, awarding her with a type of pleasure that every woman should experience at least once in their life.

The thought brought heat to London's cheeks. Their sex life had exceeded her expectations and she had experienced positions with Mason that she never thought to try with another man. Not that she had been with many men.

She continued her perusal of him. Though handsome in a nondescript way, he embodied everything male. Big, strong, and protective, the same qualities he possessed when they were younger. Asleep he seemed so harmless, but she knew better. Not only did he have the power to break her heart, but he had the power to demolish Cory.

Early in her adult life, London rarely let a man get close, choosing to date sporadically. As she got older, she felt more alone in the world, wanting ... no, needing to have someone to come home to. London wanted someone to call her own and then she met Cory.

Disgust settled in her mouth at the thought of him. How had she chosen so wrong? She'd be lying to herself if she said that she hadn't noticed early signs of his controlling nature as well as the way he sometimes disrespected her. But she still couldn't believe he hated her enough to slash her tires.

"Hey, beautiful," Mason said, his voice raspy from sleep as he stared down at her.

"Hi." She gazed into his eyes and lifted her palm to his cheek, his day-old scruff tickling her hand. All the love she felt for him was suddenly overwhelming. This sweet, thoughtful, generous man had been by her side since she returned to Atlanta. Between him and his siblings, she felt so loved. For the first time in a long time, London felt like she was finally a part of a family.

Mason touched an area above her right eye. "What are you thinking so hard about? You have creases in your forehead."

"I'm thinking about how much I love you. I'm also thinking about how much I love Harp and Cam. You guys have pulled me into your circle and—"

"You have always been a part of our circle. And before you hit me, I'm not going to say you're like a little sister. Because if you were my sister, I wouldn't be able to touch you like this."

His large hand slid slowly down the front of her body, cupping one of her breasts. Outlining the tip of her nipple with his thumb caused it to bud immediately.

London sucked in a breath and gripped his bicep when he increased the pressure. Her sex suddenly throbbed with need. After a few minutes of getting her worked up, his hand seared a path down her abdomen and went lower.

"I also wouldn't be able to touch you like this." He slipped a finger inside of her and then another.

A wave of heat shot through London's body and she whimpered, gripping his arm tighter as she arched her back.

"Mase." Her heart pounded against her ribcage while his masterful fingers glided in and out of her. She rode his hand, rocking with each stroke as his touch sent jolts of pleasure shooting through her body. "Mason," she whimpered.

"I'm right here, baby." He rolled her onto her back, not breaking contact. His fingers worked feverishly as he captured her mouth in a hungry kiss. Lips so soft and coaxing, lust shot through her like a speeding bullet, hitting her right in the core. She wanted this to last longer, but her self-control was no match against the power of his teasing touch.

Waves of ecstasy throbbed through her body as he brushed a kiss along her cheek, her neck, and then down to her shoulder. He moved back up and nibbled on her neck. Pleasure, pure and explosive swirled within her and she couldn't hold on as his fingers continued pleasuring her.

Involuntary tremors began and an orgasm ripped through her like a Tsunami crashing against the shore, washing out everything in its way. Gulping for air, she loosened her hands from Mason's huge biceps and dropped her arms to the bed, trying to catch her breath.

He nipped at her top lip and then her bottom one, not caring that he had just pulled every bit of energy out of her. Not giving her a chance to form her next thought, he positioned himself between her thighs and inched into her moist heat. She moaned as he filled her completely.

Mason started moving in and out of her as he captured her mouth in the sweetest kiss. London placed her hand behind his head and pulled him closer, passion engulfing her as they moved in perfect harmony. Their moans mingled, filling the quietness in the room. God, she loved this man and the pleasure he always gave her.

She knew she was about to climax again, feeling as if she were tiptoeing to the edge of a cliff, ready to spread her arms and soar over a gorgeous canyon. She lifted her hips and rocked with Mason as he whispered loving words into her ear. She matched his moves stroke for stroke and his pace increased; his powerful thrusts growing faster and harder.

"London, aw, baby," he groaned, his body more jerky.

She held on tight until she couldn't. An orgasm seized her body and a scream ripped from her throat. Her head thrashed against the pillow and she fell apart beneath him.

Mason was right behind her. His release was hard and commanding as he growled out her name before collapsing on top of her. As if suddenly remembering she was beneath him, he rolled to his back and pulled her to his side. Still breathing hard, he kissed the top of her head.

"I guess it's safe to say that you definitely don't think of me as a sister. And for the record, I never thought of you as my brother."

Mason chuckled. "Good to know." His eyes drifted closed.

Their sweat-slicked, naked bodies hummed from their lovemaking. London snuggled even closer to Mason, their legs intertwined. Had he realized that they hadn't used a condom? Or maybe he was like her. She realized it, but she wouldn't have been able to stop even if she wanted to. If they created a baby, wonderful. If not, that was okay, too.

Disappointment pierced London's heart. Who was she kidding? Spending the last few months with Mason, she knew without a doubt that he was the man for her. Unfortunately, she wanted way more than just his babies. She wanted all of him, which was still more than he was willing to give. This was what London wanted all the time. Not just his warm body lying next to her, but also the way he made her feel whenever they were together.

She made circles with her finger on his chest, his breathing back to normal as his snores filled the room again. Regret consumed her body. What had she been thinking? Their original plan would never be enough for her. She wanted the whole fantasy and because she'd been a fool to think she could settle for less, she might ruin what was once a special friendship.

CHAPTER TWELVE

Mason stood inside of the jewelry store, staring at the engagement ring he'd had designed for London. The elegant, heart-shaped diamond with a diamond-studded twisted band and platinum setting was perfect for her.

"Does it meet with your approval?" the sales lady asked. "If not, we can send it back to the designer and—"

"No. It's perfect."

"Great. I'm so glad you approve. I'll just need you to sign for it."

Mason followed her. He hadn't decided when he would propose to London, but he knew it would be soon. He wanted to wait until the situation with Cory had been rectified. It had been three weeks since the tire incident. Three damn weeks and no Cory. It was as if the guy had fallen off the face of the Earth.

Minutes later, Mason jogged to his truck, dashing through the steady downpour of rain. He climbed in, and his cell phone vibrated. Starting the vehicle, he activated the Bluetooth.

"Hello."

"Hey." London's sweet voice drifted through the speakers.

"Hey, baby. You ready?"

After a slight hesitation she said, "I'm already home. Can you come over?"

"What the heck? How'd you get home?" He made a U-turn and headed toward Midtown wondering what was going on. "Are you okay?"

"Yes. I got off of work early and took Uber home."

"London, why didn't you call me? I would've picked you up."

"I … can you just come over? We can talk when you get here."

Mason agreed and disconnected, all types of thoughts rolling through his mind. He gripped the steering wheel tighter as he sat impatiently at a stoplight, anxious to get to her. He couldn't believe she hadn't waited at work for him. They had an agreement—he would drop her off and pick her up every day until Cory was found. For the past three weeks, they'd fallen into a solid routine. So why hadn't she waited for him today?

Now that Mason thought about it, she had been acting strange for the last couple of days. Quieter and more distant than she'd been since the tire incident.

For the most part, everything seemed normal. They had gotten into a good rhythm and it was as if they'd lived together forever. She had even started giving him cooking lessons. And having her share his bed every night was like the icing on a cupcake.

So needless to say, Mason had been surprised when she told him a couple of days ago that she was ready to return to Harper's place. Even though Harper was back in town, and the security at the loft was tight, Mason wanted London to stay with him. He enjoyed having her close and was getting used to having her around. Had someone told him months ago that he would actually enjoy having a woman share his space, he would have laughed them out of the room.

Mason's phone vibrated and again he activated Bluetooth.

"Yeah."

"Mase, this is Larry Conner." Larry, Mason's contact in Charlotte, North Carolina, was an assistant state prosecutor. They had met years ago through a mutual friend. Larry had told Mason that he would keep him abreast of any information that came through about Cory.

"Tell me the cops found that asshole."

"Well, yeah they found him. He's dead."

Whoa. That was news Mason hadn't anticipated, but he couldn't say that he felt a lick of sympathy. "What happened?"

"The situation is still under investigation, but the police found him on the side of an apartment complex last night. He was shot to death."

"Do they have any leads?"

"They picked up a person of interest, but the guy hasn't been formally charged. Supposedly Cory was having an affair with this man's wife, but the guy hasn't admitted to killing Cory."

"Damn."

"I know, right? Well, I gotta get going. I wanted to give you an update. Once they have a few more details figured out, I'm sure someone from Charlotte's Police Department will be contacting London."

"That's cool."

Though Mason hadn't necessarily wanted the guy dead, he was glad Cory was no longer a threat to London. Now they could move on with their lives.

*

London paced the length of Harper's loft, her flip-flops squeaking against the floor. Until a few days ago, she thought she could be with Mason knowing that he had no intentions of marrying her. But after playing house with him for the past few weeks, she had fallen deeper in love. Dating him would never be enough. She wanted more.

Tonight she had to tell him that she couldn't keep going the way they were going. What had she been thinking in the first place? There was no way being the mother of his children and not his wife would be enough. She had been wrong. She wanted Mason as her husband.

She groaned and wandered into the kitchen, pulling a bottled water from the refrigerator. This was going to be the hardest conversation she'd ever had. Tonight the man she wanted to build a life with might walk out that door and want nothing else to do with her. The thought made her heart ache. Why couldn't he see that they were perfect together?

Removing the cap from the water bottle, her hands shook and water spilled over the top. Why were her hands shaking? She set the bottle down on the countertop and ripped off a paper towel to clean up her mess. *Think positive.* She and Mason had agreed that if at any point their arrangement wasn't working they would discuss it. They had always been able to talk, maybe this conversation wouldn't be as challenging as she was imagining. But what type of discussion could they really have when she went into the relationship knowing the deal. Mason had made it clear what he wanted and what he didn't want. Her misery was her fault.

London's head jerked up when there was a knock at the door.

"Tiny, open up, it's me," Mason announced from the other side of the door. Part of her didn't want to let him in, knowing that this might be the end for them. But if she didn't let him in soon, he would just use his key.

She swung the door open and he stepped across the threshold, pulling her into his arms. No words were spoken.

When Mason released her, he cupped her cheek and searched her eyes. "Why are you crying?"

She wasn't crying, but her eyes probably were a little teary.

"We need to talk." London knew men hated those words, but she didn't know what else to say. She stepped out of his arms. No way could she say what needed to be said with him touching her.

"There's something I need to tell you first," he said.

London's cell phone rang, and she glanced at the dining room table where it was sitting. Instead of answering, she returned her attention to the handsome man standing before her.

"Mason, I need to go first." She moved around the living room and then the attached dining room, unable to stand still. It felt as if her heart was literally crumbling inside of her chest.

"I can't keep going like this." Her cell phone rang again, and again she ignored it. "I love you. God, I love you so much, but—"

"London."

She lifted her hand. "Mase, please let me finish. You were right. Being the mother of your children is not going to be enough for me. I respect that you don't want more from me ... from us, but I want the whole dream. I want to be married to the father of my children. I want my babies to grow up within a family, like I once had."

London didn't have her parents long, but the years she did have them were wonderful. Not many days went by that she didn't think about them and her grandparents.

Mason stuffed his hands into the front pockets of his jeans, looking as if he was going to speak, but stopped when London's cell phone rang again.

Whoever was calling wasn't giving up.

"I'm sorry. I'd better get that. It might be the station." She swiped the phone from the table. "Hello."

"Oh thank God, I caught you." London immediately recognized her old neighbor from Charleston. "I don't know if you've heard, but Cory's dead."

London's hand went to her chest, her pulse pounding loudly in her ears. "What?"

Shock rocked her body and she looked up to see Mason moving toward her.

"Cory was shot to death outside of an apartment building. I just saw it on the news. He was shot two times. Once in the shoulder and once in the stomach."

London tuned out everything else her neighbor was saying. All London could do was stare at Mason. She vaguely remembered saying good-bye when she disconnected the call.

Mason reached for her, his hand gripping her elbow and pulling out one of the chairs. "Here, sit down."

"No." London shook her head and moved away from him. "Cory is dead. Shot two times."

Sighing, Mason lowered his head. "That was part of what I wanted to tell you when I—"

"You killed him," London said as a statement more so than a question. She knew how much he hated Cory and had threatened to go after him. "How could you? How could you do this knowing how much you have to lose? You might go to jail, and for what? He wasn't worth it!"

she yelled.

Mason's eyebrows drew together. "Wait a minute. You think I killed him?"

"Didn't you?"

"No I didn't. I might have wanted him out of your life, but I didn't do this. Besides, when would I have had a chance? I've been with you every day."

"But we haven't been spending all day together. You had time to go to North Carolina. Or you could have gotten someone else to do it." London covered her mouth with her hand, unable to believe that Mason would go so far as to kill for her. He might've ruined his life ... because of her. "I never wanted—"

"It wasn't me, London. I didn't kill him."

London said nothing, her mind spinning. Cory was dead. She wanted him out of her life, but not like this.

Mason tilted his head and narrowed his eyes. "You think I'm lying to you?"

He said the words quietly, but London didn't miss the hurt in his tone. At the moment, she wasn't sure what to believe. More than once she had heard him say he would love to get his hands on Cory. Mason had always been a hothead, especially where she was concerned, but she never thought he would kill Cory. Then again ...

"You know what? You don't have to answer. Your silence is speaking volumes."

"Mason."

"How can you claim to love someone who you don't trust?" He headed to the door, but stopped, his hand on the doorknob. He glanced over his shoulder and pinned her with a lethal glint in his eyes. "Oh, and for the record, it wouldn't have taken me two shots to kill the asshole. A bullet to the head would have done it for me."

He walked out, slamming the door behind him.

London's heart split open and she slumped into one of the dining room chairs.

"Oh, God. What have I done?"

*

Mason bypassed the elevator and took the stairs two at a time. Adrenaline and anger soared through his veins, propelling him forward like a car without brakes, flying through intersections. How the hell could she not believe him? He had done some shitty things in his life, but he would never lie to her. Never.

"I love you my ass," he growled when he reached the garage. He yanked the door open, not giving a damn that it slammed against the wall. This was why he didn't do relationships. They only came with bullshit drama. And he didn't do drama. If he had never let London get close, she never would have been able to rip out his heart.

It'll be a cold day in hell before I ever let anyone get that close again.

CHAPTER THIRTEEN

London pulled her suitcases from the walk-in closet and placed them on the bed, tears clouding her vision. She didn't want to leave Atlanta, but she didn't know what else to do. For the past week she hadn't been able to sleep or eat. She had screwed everything up with Mason and would never forgive herself for hurting him. He wouldn't take her calls. He didn't answer his door. He hadn't been at the club. If it weren't for Cameron, she wouldn't even know if Mason was dead or alive. He had called Cameron a few days ago saying that he was fine, but needed some time away.

London didn't blame him for not wanting anything to do with her. Cameron had told her to give Mason time, that he would come around. For some reason, Cameron and Harper thought that Mason loved her too much to stay away for too long. But London knew better. They hadn't seen the hurt and anger in his eyes when he walked out the door.

Breathing hard, London sat on the side of the bed trying to catch her breath. She hadn't made much progress in packing because her body was fighting her. She not only had to leave Atlanta to get her head straight regarding Mason, but she had to get her asthma under control. The humidity wasn't helping, but neither was the stress, crying, and the sleepless nights. All were probably playing a role in the flare-ups.

London ran her hands down her face, determined not to shed another tear. She glanced at the clock on the side table. *Twelve-thirty*. She'd wanted to be on the road hours ago. After not being able to fall asleep, she had finally made the decision that she needed to get out of town. A road trip to Chicago would be the perfect distraction. It was one of her favorite cities and a good place to regroup.

Needless to say her boss, Carol, the station manager, had been surprised when she called that morning to resign. She had never left a job without giving a two-week notice, but though she enjoyed the work, the hours were killing her. After a long conversation, Carol suggested London not resign, but take a few days and think about what she really wanted for her career. London wanted to hug her through the phone line. Carol always came across like a mother to many of London's co-workers and that was no different where London was concerned. When they had talked that morning, the compassion she felt from Carol's words of encouragement and support had her thinking about her mother.

"Okay, London, don't go there," she told herself. She needed to get moving. Bringing the back of her hand to her top lip, London dabbed at the perspiration forming there. Even with the air conditioner on, the room still felt muggy. She went to the closet and started removing her clothes from hangers, but her hand stalled on the red dress—the dress she had purchased solely with Mason in mind.

Her heart pounded an unsteady beat as she held the garment to her chest, emotion clogging her throat. Her life was a mess. When she had decided to move back to Atlanta, she'd high expectations. This was supposed to be the best year of her life. A new chapter. She was home. She was with the only family she had, the Bennetts, and had finally landed her dream job. Yet nothing had turned out as planned.

Unable to hold back the tears, she crumbled to the floor of the closet and sobbed. A hopelessness she hadn't felt in months washed over her. Days like this she wished she had her mother. Even though London had been young when her mother passed away, she remembered talking to her about anything. She remembered the hugs and the whispers of encouragement against her ear, letting her know that everything was going to be okay. What she wouldn't give to have her mother back.

London didn't know how long she'd been in the closet when she struggled to stand. Blowing out a ragged breath, she righted herself. The tears and self-pity had to stop. *Life goes on even after heartbreak.*

She grabbed more clothes from the closet and set them on the bed, before moving to the dresser. She still had to get her toiletries together and she wanted to wash the linens before she left. At this rate, she wouldn't get on the road until late afternoon.

"Hey, do you want to—" Harper started but stopped as she stood in the bedroom doorway eying the suitcases before walking farther into the room. "What are you doing?"

"Hey," London said. Harper had spent the day and night with Hunter, so they hadn't had a chance to talk. "I didn't realize you were home. And to answer your question, I'm getting away for a little while. But I want you to know how much I appreciate you letting me stay with you. You have truly been a godsend. I don't know what … I would have done … without you these last few months," she said between breaths, frustrated with her body. She took a sluggish breath in and blew it out slowly, unable to hold back a cough.

"I can't believe you're going to leave. Just call him. I know Mason will forgive you," Harper pleaded. "Don't leave. Don't give up on him."

"Harp, you know him. He doesn't … just forgive … and forget. You didn't see him. You didn't see … the hurt in his eyes." London leaned against the wall, her energy spent. She had been up for hours and should have been done packing. It was as if someone was siphoning the energy out of her. "Even if he did … forgive me, I can't forgive … myself for what I … did to him."

"You weren't thinking. You were in shock and I know my brother understands that. Heck, I was shocked, too, and I didn't even know Cory well."

London shook her head, immediately regretting the move. Blinking rapidly to clear her sight, she leaned against the wall again. She sucked in a breath, coughed, and tried again.

Harper might've thought that Mason understood, but his actions said otherwise. Their relationship was over. But what had London expected? First she told him that she couldn't continue carrying on the way they were, and then she basically called him a liar. Who would want to be with someone like that?

"At least don't leave until you're feeling better."

"I'll be fine. And I do feel better."

"You don't seem any better. Your skin is still pale and look at you. You can barely stand up without leaning against something." Harper moved closer, concern covering her face. London hadn't looked in the mirror since brushing her teeth that morning and could only imagine what she looked like. "And you're still having a hard time breathing. Have you even taken your medication?"

"I have." At least she had that morning. She was so distracted, the last few days had been hit or miss with the inhaler.

"You need to see a doctor."

"I will."

"Today, London. I can't believe you're even thinking about going anywhere like this. Let me call Mason. If I can't talk some sense into you, maybe he can."

"D-don't … bother. He … He's still not an … answering."

London pushed away from the wall and the room started spinning. A heaviness descended on her like a black fog and she grabbed her neck, unable to breathe.

Oh, God.

Wheezing, she pulled at the top of her shirt as if the move would force air into her lungs. Reaching out, she tried grabbing hold of the wall as tears blurred her eyes.

"London? London!"

Harper's voice sounded in the distance, but London couldn't speak. Darkness surrounded her, pushing her deeper into an abyss before being blanketed in unconsciousness.

*

"Mase, can I holler at you for a minute?" Hamilton nodded his head toward the stairs that led up to the control room. The club wouldn't open for another two hours, but Mason had called his security team in early for a meeting. "Oh and, Jack, can you order dinner and drinks for everyone who's on staff tonight?" Hamilton asked. "The rest of you can either stick around and eat or you can take off. I'll hook you up with dinner during your next shift."

"What?" Mason growled the moment they stepped into the control room and Hamilton closed the door. "What couldn't wait until after the meeting? And how you gon' just dismissed them when I wasn't even done?"

"I'm not sure where you've been for the past week, but you need to take some more time off until you get your head on straight. That wasn't a meeting down there. The way you were going off on everyone a minute ago was more like you were using each one of us as your own personal whipping boy."

Sitting on the edge of the desk that was shoved into a corner of the room, Mason folded his arms across his chest, irked by the way Hamilton was glaring at him. "So what, you're like the expert on how to run a meeting now? If I see people slacking, I'm going to let them know."

"But see that's just it. You haven't been here, Mase. How would you know if they were slacking? Some of them know you and London aren't together anymore and are giving you a pass. At some point, though, they're going to push back."

"And when they do, their ass is out of here."

"We've been tolerating your shit for the past ninety minutes. I'm about ready to leave my own damn self." Sighing, Hamilton dropped down in one of the chairs. "Listen, man, I know you're hurting and I'm sorry about you and London, but you gotta chill. Go back to wherever you've been hiding out. We've got everything covered here."

Mason said nothing as he stared down at the hardwood floor. Hurting didn't begin to describe what he was feeling. It was as if someone had reached into his chest, wrapped their hands around his heart, yanked it out, and then ran it through a meat grinder. He had never been on an emotional roller coaster like the one he experienced this past week.

Rising, he rubbed his hand over his head and down to the back of his neck. The breakup had caught him totally off guard. He knew something was up with London, but what should have been an easy conversation, had quickly turned into something he hadn't even recognized. He understood she wanted more from their relationship and he had finally been ready to take that next step. And he would have told her that had she given him the chance. Instead, she totally blindsided him.

He released an exaggerated breath and shoved his hands into the front pockets of his jeans, staring at the monitors, but not really seeing anything. In London's defense, finding out the person who had been harassing her was now dead would shock anyone. And she had good reason to believe that he would kill for her. He hadn't, but he would have. He would never forget the fear in her eyes. She had said more than once she couldn't handle if he got into trouble because of her. Unfortunately, what Mason couldn't ignore was that even after he told her he had nothing to do with Cory's death, she hadn't believed him.

Despite how pissed he was at her, she was never far from his thoughts. He had to pack a bag and leave his loft because everywhere he looked, sat, or ate, reminded him of their last few months together. Mason had taken a slow drive to Savannah, Georgia and had called Cameron to let him know that he was all right, but would be off the grid for a few days. Despite the distance he had put between him and London, he couldn't even close his eyes without seeing her angelic face. No matter how he tried to fight his feelings, he knew she was the woman for him. But he couldn't be with someone who didn't trust him.

Who was he kidding? Mason knew she trusted him. Was he using her shock as an out? Was he finding any excuse to not move forward with asking her to marry him? The only woman he had ever loved and he was walking away without a fight. He always fought for what he wanted, but this—

"You said you needed to finish up some paperwork for Supreme Security Agency-Atlanta." Hamilton interrupted Mason's thoughts. "Why not take time off and handle that?"

He was right. Mason didn't have to be there. He shouldn't be there, especially considering he still felt like punching something. Their staff was more than capable of handling the club's security and any other issues that popped up. The truth was, he was staying away from home because he still felt London's presence there. Her scent, memories of making love to her in his bed, and even her workout clothes that he'd found in his hamper. She wasn't out of his system and he feared she never would be.

"You're right. I do need to clear my head. But first I have to apologize to everyone. Just leave the dinner receipt for me. The least I can do is cover that since I made a total ass of myself down there."

"Oh, I had already planned on billing you for the meal." Hamilton chuckled. "As for your very capable staff, they know you're not yourself right now. I doubt they'll hold your behavior over your head for too long."

Mason nodded. Their employees were the best of the best when it came to security, and had shown their loyalty to him and the club from day one. "I think I'll—"

The private line rang and Hamilton quickly picked it up. "This is Ha— Wait, Harp, calm down, I ..."

The small hairs on the back of Mason's neck rose when Hamilton casted a glance at him. Mason didn't know what was going on, but a sense of doom gripped his body. Only his family and the staff had the telephone number to the control room.

"Yeah ... yeah." Hamilton stood. "He's right here."

Mason braced himself when Hamilton hung up. "Is Harp all right? What happened?"

"It's not her. It's London."

Fear like nothing Mason had ever experienced gripped his body and he grabbed hold of the edge of the console. "Wha—"

"She's been rushed to the hospital."

CHAPTER FOURTEEN

Several hours later, Mason sat next to London's hospital bed holding her hand. Harper sat near the window, while Cameron paced between them. All of them worried. London had had asthma attacks before, but Mason didn't know of a time when she had ended up in the hospital. The nurse had removed the oxygen mask over an hour ago, but London was still hooked up to an IV. Not only had she suffered an attack, but she was also dehydrated. Who knew the last time she had eaten or drank anything?

The thought had Mason remembering how he had found every excuse to feed her those first few weeks of her being back in Atlanta. She was one of those people who lost their appetite whenever she was stressed. What had he been thinking taking off like that? Sure he was angry, but a serious conversation between them would have ended this nonsense. But no. He had ignored her calls and tried to wipe the memories of her from his mind.

Mason brought London's fingers to his lips and kissed the back of them. The bandage on the side of her head stood out like a pimp in a pink fedora at a church service, taunting him, reminding Mason that he hadn't been there for her. According to Harper, London had collapsed in her bedroom, hitting her head on the wall. Thank God she didn't have a concussion, and Mason didn't even want to think about what could have happened if Harper hadn't been there.

He rubbed his forehead, his chest tight from worry. If only he had been there. Guilt swirled in his gut. She hadn't been feeling well for the last few weeks, but Mason had no idea something like this would happen. When he arrived at the hospital, Harper had reamed him out for not having his cell phone on. He couldn't ever remember his sister being that upset. She had been trying to reach him since London's incident, getting angrier by the minute. Mason had turned his cell off days ago after listening to London's third voicemail, where she had left a tearful apology. He thought falling off the grid would rid him of thoughts of her. He'd been wrong.

Harper stepped behind Mason and wrapped her arms around his neck, her chin resting on his shoulder. Her soft fragrance, similar to London's tickled his nose.

"I'm sorry I yelled at you when you got here. Even if your cell phone had been on, there was nothing you could have done."

Cameron approached the bed, his hands shoved into the front pockets of his slacks. "I'm going down to the cafeteria. You guys want anything?"

Mason shook his head. He hadn't left London's side since arriving, wanting to be there when she woke up.

"I'll go with you," Harper said.

"I'll wait for you in the hall."

After Cameron left the room, Harper leaned close to Mason's ear. "You gotta fix this, Mase. London loves you more than life and I know you feel the same way about her. Disagreements happen even in the strongest relationships, look at Mom and Dad. They argue, but they never walk out on each other. You can't just disappear."

Mason gazed up at his sister wondering if something else was going on. He had been out of the loop for a while and didn't even know if she was still dating the Hunter dude. There was something different about her, something gentler in the way she was talking to him. He had a feeling it wasn't just about London being in the hospital.

"You okay?" he asked her, pulling on the end of her hair like he used to do when they were kids. When she didn't swat his hand away or punch him, he knew that something was up. "What's going on with you?"

Her hesitation spoke volumes and then she sighed. "Nothing. I'm just worried about you guys. You and London need each other. But if you let her leave town, she mi—"

"Wait." Frowning, Mason leaned back. "She was leaving?"

Harper nodded, sadness in her eyes. "She didn't want to stay here knowing she had hurt you. Mason, fight for her if you truly love her." She placed a kiss on his cheek and hugged him before leaving.

When the door closed behind her, Mason returned his attention to London. She had been awake earlier, but only for a few minutes. Weak and out of it, Mason wasn't sure she knew he was there.

He pushed his chair away from the bed, stretching his legs out in front of him. His gaze landed on a landscape painting on the wall directly across from him. He couldn't believe London had been planning to leave. Then again, why was he surprised? He had left. He understood the need to run away.

Mason shifted his attention back to London lying eerily still. Little did she know that even if she had left, he would have hunted her down. Yeah she had ticked him off, but she was a part of him. They clearly had some work to do on their relationship, but that didn't change how much he loved her.

He stood and sat on the edge of the bed, staring down at her beautiful face wishing she would open her eyes. Caressing her cheek, a sense of calm swept over him. They were going to be okay.

"Baby, I need you." Mason placed a lingering kiss on her cheek. "And I love you."

*

London eased her eyes opened and darkness greeted her except for a hint of light to her left. Too exhausted to move her head, especially with the steady throb pounding against her skull, she just laid there. She knew she was in the hospital and had been drifting in and out of sleep, but had no idea how long she'd been there.

A heavy weight on her left hand had her wondering what she'd done to it. She struggled to move her fingers, but folded them into a fist when she felt movement. Someone squeezed her hand and then kissed it. Her heart pounded triple time when Mason's face came into view.

"Mase." A whimper crawled through her throat and tears popped into her eyes as she remembered the last time they were together. She had never been so happy to see anyone in her life.

"You're finally awake," he said, his voice heavy with sleep. "Even my kisses couldn't get you to open those gorgeous, brown eyes."

Tears dripped down London's cheek when his lips touched hers in the sweetest kiss. She never thought she'd be on the receiving end of one of his kisses again. And with the way she had treated him, accusing him of murder, she didn't deserve his gentle lips against hers. She didn't deserve him.

Knowing that didn't stop her from wanting to touch him.

Bringing her hands up to touch his face, she winced when she felt a pinch on her right hand, but she ignored the discomfort of the IV. "I'm sorry. I'm so, so sorry I didn't believe you. I heard you, but I guess I wasn't listening and I-I—" she choked out.

"Shhh, calm down before you get yourself all worked up. I just need you to get better so that I can get you the hell out of here." Mason wiped her tears with the pads of his thumbs and her eyes drifted close, soaking up his touch. "We have a lot to talk about, Tiny."

Hearing him call her Tiny pierced her heart. Thank God he was willing to talk to her. She thought for sure that they were through, that he would never speak to her again. It would have served her right. How could she have ever doubted his word?

"I love you so much." She hoped the declaration could cancel out her mistake.

"I know, baby. And I love you more. Always have. Always will." Mason kissed her again, but this time his hungry lips devoured hers as if wanting her to feel how much he loved her. She felt his emotions, thankful that they matched everything she felt within her heart.

Mason was right. They did have a lot to talk about.

The next morning, London sat up in the hospital bed as she and Mason shared breakfast. He had made a phone call the moment he received the okay that he could bring in breakfast for her. The chocolate chip waffles and hash browns were like a treat to her taste buds.

"I thought we were through with you constantly trying to feed me," she said between bites.

"I thought so to until I walked in here yesterday and saw that you had lost the weight that you had gained. I guess I'm going to have to be around you all the time to make sure you eat, even if that means going to work with you."

Mason mentioning her job reminded her of what he didn't know. Harper didn't even know.

"I'm quitting my job."

His fork stopped midair. "What? Why? I thought you liked the job. You said you always wanted to be a news anchor."

London pushed her container of food away, but Mason lifted a brow and pushed it back toward her. "I'm full."

"Try to eat a little more while you tell me why you left the job you said that you loved."

London picked up her fork and placed another bite of the waffle into her mouth. "I did love it, but I couldn't handle the hours. Some days I was so busy that I wasn't taking my medication properly and I think right now, I need a change. I also thought you and I were over. So I was planning to leave town."

Mason said nothing for the longest time. "*Was* planning. Does that mean you're staying now?"

London wasn't sure how to respond. They still hadn't really talked about their relationship. Although the fact that he had been there with her around the clock spoke volumes. Harper told her that Mason had only left for about a half an hour while London napped the day before. Other than that, he had been right by her side.

"I don't want to leave. But, Mason, I can't go back to the set up that we had. I think you would be an amazing father for my children, but I want marriage and a man I can build a life with. I want my children to grow up with a mommy and daddy in the house. You were right from the beginning when you said that our set up wouldn't be enough for me." Sighing, London looked him in the eyes. "Besides all of that, I know I won't be able to handle running into you around Atlanta."

"Even if we were married?"

London sat stunned, wondering if she had heard him correctly. "What did you say?"

When he dug through the front pocket of his jeans and pulled out a velvet box, London covered her mouth with her hands.

"This is not how I planned to ask you to be my wife, but now is as good of a time as ever. By the way, have I ever mentioned that you talk too much?"

London laughed through her tears. "You used to say it all the time when we were kids."

"These last few months with you have been some of the best months of my life. I love talking to you at the end of a work day. I love being able to sit across the table from you and share a meal. While sharing my home space with you after the tire incident, I realized how much I love having you around. I love waking up to you, even at three in the morning."

London laughed again, her love for him growing by the minute.

"And I love our relationship, especially since I was so against the idea of settling down. Hell, I even love forcing you to eat. It makes me feel as if I'm taking care of you."

"Oh, Mason." London swiped at her tears, not sure how much more of his sweet words she could take.

"I love you, Tiny. If you'll agree to be my wife, I will spend the rest of my life proving to you just how much I love you." He opened the box and a sob rattled in London's throat. "Will you marry me … and have my babies?"

"Yes!" She laughed and then squealed. "Yes, I'll marry you … and I'll have your babies."

EPILOGUE

20 months later

Mason leaned against the kitchen counter watching his son make a mess of his oatmeal. There were still times when he couldn't believe that he was a father. Each day brought with it a new adventure.

"Are you done, lil man?" His son flashed a two-teeth grin. At ten months old, Mason Jr. was taller and weighed more than most children in his age group. He'd been born a month early, but was a happy, healthy baby.

The last year and a half had been life changing for Mason. Readjusting his attitude and his life to accommodate a wife and a child hadn't been as hard as he thought it would be. For years he told himself that being in a serious relationship meant a life of drama. Boy had he been wrong. Once he changed his mindset, his life changed. He and London talked and dealt with the Cory situation and the lack of trust, as well as dealt with getting her the right medication to help better control her asthma. After those issues were handled, their relationship soared, bringing him to this moment of contentment and happiness.

Mason glanced up as London entered the kitchen. "Good morning, beautiful." He reached for her hand and pulled her to his side, kissing her lips.

Smiling, she cupped his cheek. He lived for seeing the love radiating in her eyes the way it was now. "Good morning."

"For a minute, I thought you were going to sleep the day away."

"Nope. I figured I'd better get up. I was afraid you and the munchkin were going to try making breakfast again." The cooking lessons for Mason had fallen by the wayside after he had set the kitchen on fire when he tried making her pancakes and bacon.

London ruffled Mason Jr.'s curly hair and kissed the top of his head. "How's Mommy's baby doing?" she cooed, nuzzling his neck. Covered in oatmeal, with some dripping from his mouth, he graced her with a huge grin and some babbling. "Looks like you're wearing most of your food, sweetie."

"You're right," Mason said. "I started off feeding him, but then he decided he wanted to feed himself. He kept putting his hand in the bowl and then stuffing food into his mouth."

Mason wrapped his arms around London and kissed her again. "How are you and my other two boys doing this morning?" He rubbed her belly before placing a kiss on it. At four months, she looked as if she was carrying a basketball under her shirt, instead of two babies.

"We're okay, but you don't know what we're having. They might be girls. What I am certain of, though, is that we are stopping at three kids."

"What? We're just getting started. What about my basketball team? We agreed on five."

London chuckled and pushed him away when he started kissing on her neck. "No, you wanted five. I never agreed to that. When I said I wanted children, I was thinking two or three. Not five."

Two months after Mason proposed, they'd had a small church wedding with friends and his family. He often wondered where his life would be had she not propositioned him. Like with his son, life with her was an adventure that he couldn't imagine being on with anyone else.

London nudged him. "Are you listening to me?"

"I'm sorry, baby. What did you say?"

"I asked if you wanted pancakes. Have you eaten?"

Mason chuckled. Funny how time changed people. Instead of asking her about whether or not she'd eaten, a day didn't go by without her asking him. Juggling the responsibilities at Club Masquerade, and finishing the final details of Supreme Security Agency-Atlanta, Mason was stretched pretty thin. Some days, meals weren't a priority.

"Nope, I haven't eaten, and pancakes sound good. Throw in some scrambled eggs and I'll give you a foot rub later." He wiggled his eyebrows at her, eliciting a smile, knowing his bribe wasn't much of a deal for her. Massaging her feet was practically a nightly ritual.

"Throw in a candlelight dinner, with someone else cooking, and you have a deal."

Mason laughed and Mason Jr. grinned and babbled as if he understood the conversation. "Deal."

He sat at the breakfast bar, next to the baby's high chair, debating on how to bring up something that he and

London needed to discuss. He watched as she moved easily around the kitchen.

"We're going to have to start looking for a larger place. In a few months, the loft is going to get real small, real quick, especially with three boys."

London frowned. "Don't you want a little girl?"

"No." He stood when the baby started whining. Reaching into the refrigerator, Mason grabbed the bottle that he had prepared earlier and handed it to his son.

"How can you just say no without even thinking about it?"

"I have thought about it. And no, I don't want a daughter. Only sons."

"Why?"

"Because if you think I'm protective of you, how much worse will I be with daughters?"

"Good point, but don't rule out the idea." She smiled when he narrowed his eyes at her.

"Why? Do you know something I don't know?" He stood behind her and rubbed her belly.

"I'm just sayin'. I think I see a baby girl in our future." Pulling away, she opened the refrigerator and took out the carton of eggs.

"Does that mean you know what we're having? Because for the record, I'll be happy with boys or girls."

Now she was the one wiggling her eyebrows before smiling again. "Nah, I don't know, but I'm just saying don't rule out the possibility."

The idea of a little girl who looked just like London brought a smile to his face. But then he shook the thought free when he remembered that having girls meant they'd be dating boys, which was something he definitely didn't want to deal with.

Leaning his back against the breakfast bar, Mason folded his arms across his chest. "Let's go back to the original conversation. We need a bigger place." After marrying, London had moved into his loft. But now that Mason Jr. was starting to walk, the fact that they needed a bigger home was more apparent.

London said nothing. Each time he brought up the idea of them moving into a house, she shut the conversation down.

"Baby, I know how you feel, but I promise you, I'll keep you and the kids safe."

She sighed and moved over to the griddle, flipping a couple of pancakes. "I know you will try, Mason, but there are no guarantees that you can stop a home invasion."

The number of home invasions in Atlanta were growing at a startling rate, but Mason refused to let her keep living in fear. He had already taught her how to handle a gun, but that hadn't been enough to change her mind. Even after seeing a therapist for six months shortly after they were married, she still harbored some fear.

"What if we purchased a property with some land outside of the city? I'll make sure that it's gated, we'll have a state of the art alarm system, and if needed, I'll hire an armed guard to be on the property when I'm not home." There was nothing he wouldn't do to ensure the safety and happiness of his family.

Raising her gaze, London studied him. "You would do all of that just to convince me to move into a house?"

Mason approached her and pulled her into his arms, kissing the top of her head. "Baby, there is nothing I wouldn't do for you. You know that."

"I know." She looped her arms around his waist, which was getting harder to do as the babies continued to grow. Laying her head against his chest, she released a noisy sigh. "You take such good care of us. And I know you're right about us needing a larger place."

She had told him on more than one occasion that she wanted a big house with a large yard for their children. But whenever they started the process of looking, she'd change her mind.

"Why don't I call a realtor and we can start searching this weekend?"

Seconds ticked by before she lifted her head, a smile ghosting on her lips. "Okay."

His brows shot up. "Okay? You sure?"

She nodded just as Mason Jr. started banging his empty bottle on the tray of his high chair.

"It's time." She raised up on tiptoe and kissed Mason's lips. "I'm ready. I'm so grateful for our little family. I want our children to have plenty of room to run around in a backyard of their own. Most importantly, I don't want to transfer my fears to them. You don't have to go as far as hiring an armed guard, but everything else sounds good."

"Consider it done." He captured her mouth in a heated kiss. He'd been right about kissing her becoming his favorite past-time. She got sweeter as the days went by.

"I love you," he mumbled against her lips.

"I love you more."

*

Coming Soon by Sharon C. Cooper

Jenkins & Sons Construction Series, a spinoff of the Jenkins Family Series is coming soon! Of course you'll be able to catch up with the Jenkins' women, but you'll also get to journey with the Jenkins' men as they find love.

Atlanta's Finest Series – Atlanta's finest was first mentioned in A Passionate Kiss. You'll get to catch up with some reader's favorites in this series, including Malik & Natasha, Wiz & Olivia, as well as Mason & London.

***

Sharon's Email Mailing List

To get sneak peeks of upcoming stories and to hear about giveaways that Sharon is sponsoring,
join her email mailing list. www.sharoncooper.net.

***

Check out the other two books in The Bennett Triplets Series

A Passionate Love by Delaney Diamond

Simone Brooks and Cameron Bennett should not be together. She's a wealthy socialite looking for a suitable husband. A man with the right pedigree and an economic status that matches her own. He's part owner of the hottest nightclub in Atlanta with his siblings. Someone who loves cooking, the outdoors, and women, not necessarily in that order.

After one night together, their sizzling chemistry makes it difficult to stay away. Then comes the hard part—navigating their differences to salvage a relationship that, while it may be imperfect, overflows with love and passion.

A Passionate Night by Candace Shaw

Mixing business with pleasure leads to a passionate night …

Harper Bennett's motto is work hard, play hard. Lately, she's forgotten the latter and has focused her time as part-owner, along with her brothers, of the hottest nightclub in Atlanta. When an intriguing client enters, Harper forgoes her promise to never date a man that doesn't live in the same city and she finds herself playing hard to get with Hunter Arrington. The passion that has ignited between them can't be extinguished, and she dreads the day he has to leave.

Hunter travels the world because of his career and has no intentions of settling down until his eyes land on Harper. There's something about the petite, sassy woman that he adores and makes him feel at home for the first time in years. Now he's faced with a life-changing decision and the thought of being without Harper isn't an option.

Other Titles by Sharon C. Cooper:

Jenkins Family Series (Contemporary Romance)
Best Woman for the Job (Short Story Prequel)
Still the Best Woman for the Job (book 1)
All You'll Ever Need (book 2)
Tempting the Artist (book 3)
Negotiating for Love – (book 4)
Seducing the Boss Lady – (book 5)

Reunited Series (Romantic Suspense)
Blue Roses (book 1)
Secret Rendezvous (Prequel to Rendezvous with Danger)
Rendezvous with Danger (book 2)
Truth or Consequences (book 3)
Operation Midnight (book 4)

Stand Alones
Something New ("Edgy" Sweet Romance)
Legal Seduction (Harlequin Kimani – Contemporary Romance)
Sin City Temptation (Harlequin Kimani – Contemporary Romance)
A Dose of Passion (Harlequin Kimani – Contemporary Romance)
Model Attraction (Harlequin Kimani – Contemporary Romance)

About the Author

Award-winning and bestselling author, Sharon C. Cooper, is a romance-a-holic - loving anything that involves romance with a happily-ever-after, whether in books, movies, or real life. Sharon writes contemporary romance, as well as romantic suspense and enjoys rainy days, carpet picnics, and peanut butter and jelly sandwiches. She's been nominated for numerous awards and is the recipient of an Emma Award for Romantic Suspense of the Year 2015 (Truth or Consequences), Emma Award - Interracial Romance of the Year 2015 (All You'll Ever Need), and BRAB (book club) Award - Breakout Author of the Year 2014. When Sharon is not writing or working, she's hanging out with her amazing husband, doing volunteer work or reading a good book (a romance of course). To read more about Sharon and her novels, visit www.sharoncooper.net

Connect with Sharon Online:

Website: http://sharoncooper.net
Facebook:
http://www.facebook.com/AuthorSharonCCooper21?ref=hl
Twitter: https://twitter.com/#!/Sharon_Cooper1
Subscribe to her blog:
http://sharonccooper.wordpress.com/
Goodreads:
http://www.goodreads.com/author/show/5823574.Sharon_C_Cooper
Pinterest: https://www.pinterest.com/sharonccooper/

Made in the USA
San Bernardino, CA
28 September 2016